W9-BPS-088

Lisa Bunker

Felix Yz

PUFFIN BOOKS

PUFFIN BOOKS
An imprint of Penguin Random House LLC
375 Hudson Street
New York, New York 10014

First published in the United States of America by Viking,
an imprint of Penguin Random House LLC, 2017
Published by Puffin Books, an imprint of Penguin Random House LLC, 2018

THE LIBRARY OF CONGRESS HAS CATALOGED THE VIKING EDITION AS FOLLOWS:
Names: Bunker, Lisa, author.
Title: Felix Yz / Lisa Bunker.
Description: New York : Viking, [2017]. | Summary: Thirteen-year-old Felix Yz
chronicles the final month before an experimental procedure meant to
separate him from the fourth-dimensional creature, Zyx, with whom he
was accidentally fused as a young child.
Identifiers: LCCN 2016029068 | ISBN 9780425288504 (hardback)
Subjects: | CYAC: Schools—Fiction. | Family life—Fiction. | People with
disabilities—Fiction. | Extraterrestrial beings—Fiction. |
Blogs—Fiction. | Science fiction. | BISAC: JUVENILE FICTION / Family /
Alternative Family. | JUVENILE FICTION / Science Fiction.
Classification: LCC PZ7.1.B864 Fel 2017 | DDC [Fic]—dc23 LC record available
at https://lccn.loc.gov/2016029068

Puffin Books ISBN 9780425288511

Printed in the United States of America
Book design by Jim Hoover

1 3 5 7 9 10 8 6 4 2

For Cy and Sam, with love.

Thank you, Bairns, for words and art!

29 Days to Go

I almost talked to Hector today.

How it happened was, as soon as I got off the bus Tim the Bore popped up like he was waiting for me. I can't remember a time when Tim was not picking on me. He is such a jerk. Anyway, nothing new today, same old joke. "Hey, Felix," he says. "Guh-guh-guh-guess what?" Making fun of how Zyx makes it hard for me to talk. So incredibly clever, he is. As usual I don't answer, but that never stops him. "Time for the word of the day," he says. "What do you think? Will the streak continue? Let's find out. . . ." He's run-hopping along next to me, and I just stare at the ground and keep walking. "The word of the day is, Felix Yz a . . . retard!" Which is supposed to be funny because my last name sounds like "is." Get it? Then he does a leap with his arms in the air and screams, "Yes! The streak continues!"

Like I said, usually I don't respond, but this time maybe I'm feeling a little more stressy than usual on account of how hard it has been getting to move in the morning and ZeroDay finally being set, because all of a sudden I feel this hot squirt in my stomach and I make a fist. I only do it for a second before uncurling my hand again, but he still goes nuts. "What? What's that?" he shouts, shoving me and punching my shoulder. I start shaking and turn to face him, but before I can do anything else he pushes me into the janitor's closet and slams the door. I crash into the big square sink and fall over against the rolling bucket and lie there for a second, feeling swoopy.

Once the floor stops pitching around I get up and try to open the door. It pushes out a little and then slams back, and I hear Tim's stupid laugh and figure out from the foot shadows under the crack that he and one of his stupid friends must be holding the door shut. I try again and they push back so hard they make it bang. I still feel dizzy, so I slide down and sit leaning against the door, letting my body curl naturally into the Pose, the way it always wants to these days. The wood feels cool against the side of my head. They start whisper-calling through the door, but I can't hear what they're saying and I don't care.

I start to think maybe I'll take a nap or something when I hear high heels and a teacher's voice. Tim answers, and even through the door I can hear the fakey apologizing tone in his voice. The teacher speaks again and sneakers go away, squeaking hard on purpose, and then the door opens and Mrs. O is there.

Mrs. O is OK, I guess. She talks to me like I'm eight years old, but then she talks to all the other kids the same way, so maybe it's not because she thinks I'm stupid. Maybe it's because she always says things right out of the Positive Things for Teachers to Say Handbook. "Felix," she says, in her *very concerned* voice. "Are you all right?" But I hardly hear her, because Hector is standing right behind her.

OK, do I really have to explain about Hector? Because it's complicated and I don't actually know what I'm explaining and I don't want to.

do what you want do not do what you do not want

Great, Zyx, that's such a big help.

sarcasm question mark

No, you think?

sarc Yes, sarcasm. Gah. Anyway, I think I do have to explain, because that was my idea with this secret blog or e-journal or whatever, that I am telling everything from scratch to a total stranger, so that if ZeroDay goes, um . . . let's just say, if I don't happen to be around later, people will have everything they need to understand. So. Explaining Hector.

felix explain question mark

I'm thinking, I'm thinking. Uh.

Yeah, you know what? I'm done for today.

zyx love felix

You love everybody and everything. Or so you keep saying. But, yeah, thanks.

welcome

Twenty-nine days until ZeroDay. I'm counting down. Twenty-nine days to go.

28 Days to Go

I just read through what I wrote last night, and I realized that if someone reads this who doesn't know me, which is the whole idea, then there are a bunch of things that would be hard to understand, like how a lot of the time I have trouble talking, and the part about it getting hard to move in the morning, and ZeroDay, and the Pose, and the words in italics. Well, all of these things have one reason behind them, which is that when I was little there was an accident with a secret machine my dad was working on, and I got fused at the atomic level with a hyperintelligent being from the fourth dimension. Zyx, say hello.

why say hello question mark

If you understood humans better it would be easy to explain, but you don't, so it's not. Could you just do it, please?

Thank you. As you can see, Zyx communicates by using my fingers to type, but has never figured out about shift keys or punctuation. Or italics for that matter. Those I go back and put in after so you can tell who is who.

So that's Zyx (rhymes with "six," in case you were wondering), and the Pose is the exact position I was in when the accident happened. That was when I was three, so I hardly remember anything about it, but from what they tell me, Dad had me at the lab, babysitting while he worked. There were these two big spheres, and the idea of the experiment was to make a tiny crystal marble disappear from one of the spheres, pass through the fourth dimension (the actual space kind of fourth dimension, not time), and appear instantly in the other sphere, and what happened was, the machine went off before it was supposed to. Maybe Dad got a little excited or something. Mom says he could be like that—overeager is the word she used. In any case, the spheres were not sealed up the way they were supposed to be, and at that moment they figure I was losing my balance and falling on my butt, because in the Pose I'm half curled between standing and sitting, with my right arm sticking out to the side and my neck bent. Which is why I walk hunched over, and why I sleep on a recliner instead of a bed. And being fused with Zyx also makes it hard for me to talk most of the time, which is why Tim came up with the R-word for his little game. Most people think I'm mentally disabled, but I'm not. Just stuck together with an alien.

What else? ZeroDay, right. That's when the Procedure is going to happen, which means they are going to try to separate me and Zyx again. Dr. Yoon is worried that if we stay fused together for too long it might be bad for me, for both of us. None of this has ever happened before, so nobody really knows for sure, but it seems like, um . . . like . . . I don't want to say it, but I guess I have to. It seems like if we stay fused together for too long, there's a chance we might both die.

yes no

I just had to go into the bathroom for a minute and close the door. That was no fun to type.

no yes

Yeah, I see you there being all mystical, but, later. There's a chance the Procedure might kill us too, but they think the chance of that happening is much lower, so it seems best to do it. And that's without them knowing about how sometimes these days I feel frozen up in the morning, because I haven't told anyone, so when Mom said they wanted to set a date, I said OK.

How can I be thinking about stuff like this? I'm not even old enough to get my own phone yet, according to the ridiculous Mom rules in this house. And I only just got started on Jarq. I'm not nearly ready to start drawing it, not for real. How can I plan my comic about the world I'm building when my life might be about to end? Excuse me. Bathroom again.

OK, I'm back. And I think I've explained everything. So, Hector.

Um.

Gah, OK, fine. Hector is this boy at school. He's the same age as me—we're both in eighth grade—and he's one of the only students in the whole school who ever talks to me like I'm not stupid. And he laughed once when I made a joke. Laughed at the joke, I mean, not at me. And he's wicked cute and I, you know, kinda like him, so when I see him I feel like my head is suddenly full of so much blood I can't hear and I think of all these bits of things but nothing whole to say and feel like the most idiotic person on the whole planet Earth.

felix heart glow when hector look

It does not. Mind your own fourth-dimensional business.

. . .

Thank you. (The three dots, btw, that's Zyx's way of saying "no comment.") So, ANYWAY, back to what happened yesterday with Tim the Bore, et cetera, Hector is there behind Mrs. O. I guess he was just walking by, and there are a couple of other kids too, staring at me, but Hector isn't staring, he's looking concerned, and as I get to my feet he does big eyes at me and touches the side of his face with his hand. It's a mirror image of where my head hurts from hitting the sink, so I touch and feel the stickiness of blood. I do NOT want to go to the nurse and have there be this big fuss, so I keep my face turned away from Mrs. O and say, "I'm fine," trying to make it sound true. "Are you sure?" she says, and she reaches to turn me toward her, but I pull away, and then before she can try again, Ms. C comes up.

Oh, great, I think, why not just get the whole school out here, but I'm also glad to see her, because if Hector is one of the students who treats me the closest to normal, Ms. C is one of the teachers who does. When she looks at me I see—OK, this is going to sound kinda gross, but I don't mean it that way—I see her brain behind her eyes, looking in through my eyes to my brain, so there's this brain-to-brain connection. "Felix," she says, "are you all right?" "Yes," I say, tired of repeating myself, and wishing they would all go away except Hector, because the bell is going to ring any second and right at this moment I feel like I could actually almost talk to him. And just as I think that, the bell rings.

Mrs. O seems to make up her mind. "Well, all right, if you're sure," she says, already looking back over her shoulder as she click-clacks away on her high heels. I shift my feet with the idea of maybe possibly taking a step toward Hector, but then Ms. C takes my arm. She turns me and looks at the side of my head and makes a "tch" noise. "Felix, you should go to the nurse," she says. "Or at least wash that off before you go to class."

"OK, Ms. C," I say. Hector is edging away. Now I just want to leave.

"And, Felix, one more thing," she says. "I have something I want to speak with you about. Would you come to my room after school, please?"

"OK, Ms. C," I say again, feeling like a marionette, head on a string, up down up down. She lets me go and I stumble into the bathroom, wash the cut, and then go to math. I'm still feeling queasy from hitting the sink, plus now I'm wondering what kind of trouble I am in. All I can think of is that she's been chosen to tell me that all my teachers are annoyed about how I'm always drawing in class. But I have to, because I feel like I'm never going to get the character design right for Jarq unless I work on it all the time.

Speaking of trouble, I guess Tim gets into it, because after third period he walks past me in the hall with his face all glowery and his shoulders hunched, and when he sees me he gives me a look like his eyes are the twin holes in the end of a shotgun. The look says as plainly as saying the words, "I am going to KILL you." Great. I wish he would die and leave me alone.

27 Days to Go

I didn't end up going to Ms. C's room yesterday because Mom was picking me up right after school, but I met her in the hall again today and she asked me again to come see her. Since she had now asked me twice I figured I had to go, so after last bell I went to her room.

I had Ms. C for English last year. I go to regular classes and I do all right, but most of the teachers skip over me after the first few days because of how Zyx makes me talk and move. Not Ms. C. She never stopped calling on me the whole year long. She also gave me mostly good grades, and when she didn't, I understood why. She was nice to me. Still, she's a teacher, and if you are due for trouble, she has no trouble dishing it out.

Zyx, will you help me remember? There was a lot of talk. Can you do the thing where I kinda half give you control of my fingers, and you do that word-for-word recall that you do?

yes

Cool, thanks.

welcome

So I knock on the open door and she looks up from her desk and says, "Oh, good, please come in, Felix," which sounds promising. I shuffle up to her desk and stand there with my eyes down. We are the only two people in the room. "How's your head?" she asks.

I turn my face to show her. It really was just a scratch, already healing over. "Fine," I say.

"Good." There's a little pause. "Felix, I asked you to come see me because last Friday, Mr. M showed me a book report you turned in to him last week. Do you know the one I mean?"

"Yeah, sure," I say. I had been wondering about that, because he handed them back but didn't give me mine, and I wanted to see what grade I got. It was about that story with Meg and

Charles Wallace and the Echthroi. It's the first book we've read all year that I liked, so it's the first book report I tried to do a good job on.

"He asked me if . . ." She pauses, and I glance up. She looks . . . embarrassed? That seems to be how she's looking, but I can't think why. "He asked me if I thought, based on having had you in my class last year, that you actually wrote it. He thought maybe you had . . . gotten it from somewhere." I keep my face down. Mr. M is definitely one of the teachers who treat me like I'm stupid.

"Do you know what I told him?"

"No."

"I told him that I was certain you had written it, and that I thought it was well written. I told him I was sure because I recognized your voice."

Now I really look up, because, A, it sounds like I might not be in trouble after all, and, B, I don't know what she means about my voice.

"I don't know if you realize it, Felix," she says, "but you have a strong writing voice. You write clearly, and you have good ideas and you express them in a way that makes me feel like a particular person is speaking to me, and you use solid, concrete details that make what you're saying come alive. That's what I mean by a strong writing voice."

I stand there breathing for a moment and then say, "OK?"

She holds out a piece of paper. "This is an entry form for the annual Littlefield School District essay contest," she says. "There are prizes for the best essays in each age group. How old are you?"

"Thirteen."

"Then you are in the third bracket from the top, and the prize in that bracket is"—she looks at the paper—"two hundred dollars. The deadline is only two weeks from now, but that's enough time to do a good job if you get started right away. I think you should enter. I think you are a good writer, and I think you could win."

My hand reaches out by itself and takes the paper. "OK, thank you," I say, like a computerized voice, not knowing what to think. Then I turn around and walk out, still not knowing what to think, and now I'm home, and I STILL don't know what to think.

I don't want to write another stupid paper, that's for certain. But it sure would be amazing to win that two hundred dollars. Look at these topics, though. I have to pick one. "Invent a new personal philosophy and then demonstrate how your philosophy explains something important about life or the world." Are they crazy? What kind of essay topic is that?

zomboid blippian

Oh, you remember that, do you? Of course you do, you remember everything. But that's just a joke.

joke question mark

Gah, not that again. I've given up trying to explain jokes to you.

. . .

Yeah. But now that you've brought it up, I guess I have to explain. Zomboid Blippian is a thing Bea and I made up with Grandy. Zomboid means when you look inside them, all human beings have equally delicious pulsing gray brains, so why not treat them all the same? And Blippian means life is going to be over so fast anyway, we might as well be nice to each other. Or something like that. But I don't want to write a paper about it.

Anyway, one good thing about Ms. C's essay contest: I have spent almost no time today worrying about ZeroDay. I guess maybe Mom has a point, going on the way she does about still doing normal things. Normal, whatever that means.

26 Days to Go

I've been thinking about what Ms. C said about details in writing, and I've also been thinking about ZeroDay and the possible reader later, so I want to try to write about my family. I'm going to describe Dinner at the Yz Place, the dinner that just happened an hour ago.

Before I get started, though, I feel like I need one of those . . . whadayacallems? Zyx, remember at the beginning of the play we read in English, there was that list of characters with descriptions? What was that called?

dramatis personae

Yeah, that! Cool. OK, here's the dramatis personae.

Grandy. Grandy is my grandparent—one of my father's

parents—but I don't know if vo is my grandmother or my grandfather, because each week vo spends Thursday, Friday, and Saturday wearing jeans and button shirts and boots and a cap with veir hair tucked up inside, talks in a low, loud voice, and goes by Vern. Then on Sunday, Monday, and Tuesday vo dresses in frilly blouses and skirts and panty hose with veir hair brushed out soft and loose, talks in a high, soft voice, and goes by Vera. And on Wednesdays vo stays in veir room and doesn't eat and doesn't talk and doesn't wear any clothes and meditates all day. At least, that's what vo says. I really don't need to see ven naked (no offense, Grandy), so I don't ever try to open the door.

Other than that, vo's a word geek and loves to knit, as Vera and Vern both. And what else? Well, the V-words, I should explain those. Those are the pronouns Grandy invented for veirself. Instead of he him his his himself or she her her hers herself, you get vo ven veir veirs veirself. As in, vo owns it. It belongs to ven. It's veir thing. It's veirs. Vo said so veirself. And a cool thing about these V-words is that they come in handy for Zyx too, since they don't seem to have she and he over there in the fourth dimension. Hey, Zyx, are you a girl fourth-dimensional alien or a boy fourth-dimensional alien?

question mark

Yep, thought so.

Bea. Short for Beatrix. (All the names in my family end with X, to make it XYZ with our last name. It's a tradition. I roll my eyes.) Bea is my big sister, and she's medium-tall with long dark hair, and she's a piano genius. She's three years older than me, so she's a junior, and she has already gotten into this super-fancy music school where she'll be going next year instead of doing her senior year of high school. She spends about five hours a day practicing, during which she disappears so far inside the music that you can go right up to her and say her name and she won't hear you. If you want to talk to her you have to touch her, and then she might flail or snarl. And even when she's not playing the actual piano, she's usually staring off into space and playing invisible piano on whatever happens to be in front of her.

Besides the piano playing, Bea is just a sister, I guess. She's smart and does well in school and has friends and stuff. She's fun to be with sometimes, and she's a pain in the butt other times. It would be more boring if she wasn't around, so I'm glad she's part of the family.

And then there's Mom. What can I say about Mom? She's a regular-looking woman who wears regular-looking clothes.

She has light brown hair that she usually wears pulled back, but some of it always escapes again and floats around her head, and a lot of the time the fingers of one of her hands are playing with the strands hanging down by her neck. Her name is Margo, without an X. (Grandy taught me the way to spell it with an X, Margaux, but Mom wasn't born into the Yz family, she married in, so the fact that there's an ends-with-X way of spelling her name is only a coincidence.) She works at a lawyer's office, but she's not a lawyer—some kind of helper job—and she, you know, runs the house and looks after us. She's the Parent on Duty. Sometimes she gets stressy and nags, but other times she's really funny. Also, sometimes she makes treats or gets us all out doing something fun, but other times she gets really sad and I think she still misses my dad a lot, because when the accident happened, he got killed.

Um, yeah. I didn't mention that before. When the machine went off, the force field or whatever spread out in the lab like a little sun, and lucky for me I was farther away and only got fused, but he was right at the center of the sun and got vaporized. They never found anything but a little bit of the sole of one of his shoes.

Huh. You might think it would shake me up, typing that, but it doesn't. I never really knew him. I actually feel worse about him being gone for Mom than I do for myself. Is that weird? I don't know, it's just how it is. So that's Mom.

and felix

You mean, I should dramatis my own persona too? Yeah, OK, sure. I'm Felix, and I'm just a person. If it wasn't for the fused-with-Zyx thing, I suppose I would just be normal—whatever that means. And I like to draw. That's all I have to say about me.

say more

But how am I supposed to see myself?

dance self dance other see all see self

Whatever that means. Typical. But, all right, if I could split myself in two and also be standing in the corner watching, I guess I'd see a skinny kid with dark hair hanging down that he hides his eyes behind, not sitting up real straight. The parts of him that are touching the chair are his tailbone, right on the edge, and the backs of his shoulders, pressing back. Not exactly good manners, but I get so tired of pushing against the Pose. And what else? Well, I've got an almost but not quite perfect triangle of moles on my left cheek, and sometimes when

I'm thinking or distracted or whatever, I put my thumb and my first two fingers on them and then basically play drums. My fingers do all these rhythms, and maybe partly that's Zyx?

sometimes yes

Yeah, I thought so. I call it kerbopping the triangle. I don't usually do it at mealtime, though.

The only other thing to say is that an actual dinner with everyone together at the table is pretty rare at our house, because usually at least one of us has a practice or a lesson or a meeting or dinner at a friend's house or whatever. But besides her idea about still doing normal things, Mom also has this idea about the family spending as much time together as possible, so tonight there we were, all four of us around the table in the actual dining room, under the silly five-electric-candles chandelier. It was a little awkward, because we are out of the habit, but nice too.

four is three is two is one is all

If you say so.

So at first the conversation is just how was your day, fine, what did you learn at school, nothing, and then there is a pause that gets long, and then Grandy (in Vern mode, it being Friday—with suspenders) looks around the table and says, "This is lovely. It makes me wish Ajax were here." Ajax is, was, my dad.

I look at Mom, because sometimes she wants to talk about Dad and sometimes she doesn't. She appears to be pretending she didn't hear.

Bea tucks her hair behind her ear and says, "I remembered something new about him." She was six when the accident happened.

Grandy says, "Oh yes?"

"I remember he would lie on the floor and I would come running up to his feet, which had socks on, and I would run into his socks with my tummy and he would catch my hands and swing me up so I was over him."

Mom looks up.

"And then he would straighten his legs and let go of my hands and I would put them out like wings and arch my back and look up at the ceiling and really feel like I was flying."

Mom does a little twitch of a smile. "And me watching with

my heart in my mouth as you wobbled around up there. At least at first. But I got used to it, because he never dropped you."

I say, "Did he ever do that for me?" I have to ask because I don't remember much about him at all—just sort of an idea of a face, and once sitting on his lap, listening to a story with the rumble of his voice making my body vibrate, feeling all warm and safe.

Mom says, "I'm not sure. I think so. You were still awfully small, though."

Grandy says, "He doted on you both. He loved being a parent."

Mom is looking sad, so Bea puts her hand on her heart and sings, "Feels. Feels with wheels." Then she looks at me, like, Your turn.

OK, this is a thing in my family: we make up songs. Sometimes the song falls apart, but sometimes it comes together, and this is one of those times. On the beat, I sing back to her, "Over you it steals . . . this feeling of feels . . ."

Bea smiles and does opera arms and comes back in while Grandy puts a little beatbox under, which vo's really good at.

I have an odd grandparent. Anyway. "Oh, those feels!" Bea sings. "Sneak into your heart, tear it all apart, leave you gasping and sore," which is a total present of a rhyme setup, and she catches my eye, so I come back in: "But wanting more . . ." She smiles wider and nods and we find the duet: "More feels . . . Feels . . . with . . . wheels!" and on the last couple of notes, Mom finds a third note between Bea's high one and my low one, and Grandy does a duh-duh-duh-dum-doo-pshhh to finish, and we sit there grinning at each other.

"That was a good one," says Mom.

Bea says, "I like how it sounds with the third voice. Two voices are cool, but three voices are cooler."

"The middle voice," Mom answers. "Like I'm the middle generation here at this table."

That makes me think of something, and I say, "Behold, the threeness of things."

25 Days to Go

Last night in the middle of typing I got called down to take out the garbage, and then a bunch of other stuff happened to keep me downstairs until it got too late to finish, and now here it is a day later, so if anyone was reading this every day, vo would've been waiting a whole day for the rest. I made a cliffhanger. Cool.

Picking up from what I said about the threeness of things: I'm just saying it to be funny, but Grandy gives me a look. "Oh my, yes," vo says. "That's something. There *is* a threeness to things. It's a magical number. The Holy Trinity in Christian belief; the thesis, antithesis, and synthesis of the dialectic system in philosophy . . ." I have no idea what vo is talking about, but I interrupt, or Zyx does, by making my whole body jump like I just got an electric shock.

yes yes yes three in all three three three sing all help all feel all dance all is all three be not be difference between Whoa, hold it!

. . .

Thank you. Yes, I know, this is obviously exciting to you, and that's fine. I'm interested too, actually. I want to say something more about it. But let me finish telling my story first, would you please?

yes wait

Thank you. So I'm doing my Zyx-wants-to-say-something flopping routine, and normally I would go to the computer so vo could say it, but before I can Bea does that ooh-ooh-ooh thing with her hands and says, "Ooh ooh ooh! This totally reminds me of the Bach I'm working on for my recital. May I piano-geek out for you for a minute? Please please?"

"But of course," says Grandy, and Mom just smiles, the really soft happy smile I love so much from her. Bea is already up out of her chair and practically runs through the archway into the living room. The piano is right there on the other side of the wall.

"OK," she says, calling to us because she's out of sight around the corner. "This one won't be in the recital, but I need to play it for you first so you get the difference. It's a Bach two-part invention, a practice piece for teaching your hands to work independently from each other. And if you listen, you can hear it has two separate, equal voices." Then she plays a piece I remember from when I was about nine and she was about twelve. It's fast and has lots of notes, but it's not very long, maybe thirty seconds total. And I can hear what she said—there are two voices, and they weave together to make the music. Sometimes one voice is busy and the other is simple. Then they switch. Then, just to be different, they both get busy at the same time. It's really cool.

"So that's two voices," Bea says. "But he also wrote three-part pieces, and the amazing thing is that he called the two-part ones 'inventions,' like, you know, a useful little machine or something, but he called the three-part ones 'sinfonias,' like, OK, this is serious. This is three voices, so this is a symphony." She laughs. "A tiny one, but still."

Then she plays one of the pieces she's practicing now. Before, it has always seemed to me to be just a spaghetti-tangle of notes, but now I can hear that there are three separate voices. And it does kinda sound a little like a symphony. The first song sounded a little empty, like the frame of a house before the walls go up, but this one sounds full and rich.

I start to jerk and jolt again as she finishes, and judging from how my legs are jumping, Zyx wants me to get up, so I stagger into the other room. I hear Grandy's voice behind me: "Remarkable, dear. But not as remarkable as the fact that you have apparently just grown a third hand."

Bea laughs. "No, silly," she says. "That's what makes it so fun to play. You have to do the third voice in the middle with, mostly, the thumbs and the first two fingers of both hands." Then she looks up at me and says in a quieter voice, "What?"

"I think Zyx wants to see," I say through my clenched teeth. You must have been really excited.

yes yes yes three voices middle voice sing dance three three three

"OK," says Bea, and she plays the piece again, more slowly, and my body goes absolutely still, like Zyx is frozen, vo's concentrating so hard. Then as soon as she's done I start flailing again and Bea gets it and moves over, and when I sit down Zyx jerks my hands up on the keyboard and my fingers play something that seems like it might be part of what she did.

There are a lot of mashed notes, but Bea is watching and nodding and says when I stop, "Yes, Zyx, that was right. That was the middle voice." Then Zyx makes my hands jump—clang!—which I guess means, "Yay!"

yes yay middle voice pretty zyx love middle voice

OK, this has gotten long enough. But there's one more thing I want to say. That competition essay—maybe I could write about the threeness of things. The idea has gotten into my head and it's bouncing around like a ball in a pinball machine, lighting everything up. And I don't mean Zyx, though obviously vo likes it too *yes yes yes*

Yes. So, maybe. I need to think about it a bit more.

24 Days to Go

Imagine if you could cut the world in half like an orange. Not just the dirt and rock part, but the oceans and atmosphere too. Then imagine if you could cut one of the halves again, right next to the first cut, so that you got a big round slice of world thinner than paper, with layers of water on some parts and a bigger circle of air all around. Then imagine if you pressed this slice of world between two huge invisible plates of glass, so that the slice had no thickness at all anymore. On this slice you would still have gravity, which means there would still be down and up, and there would still be back and forth on the surface too, but you wouldn't be able to go around anything anymore. If you lived there, or if a slice of you did, and if slice-of-you was trying to get somewhere, you would have only over, under, or through.

That's Flatworld. Grandy told me stories about it when I was paralyzed after the accident. Vo sat by my bed every day and talked to me. I remember not being able to move or speak and being so scared that I felt like I was going insane, but when Grandy talked to me I felt less scared, so I guess I owe ven a lot.

And nobody knew it at the time, but besides helping me not go insane, vo was teaching Zyx to speak English. As much as Zyx does speak English, anyway. Or any language. I get the feeling words were a new thing for you. Do they even have words in your dimension?

not words dance

Uh-huh, right. But you can still remember every single word you've ever heard. It must be like having a collection of moon rocks or something.

. . .

Good answer. Anyway, the reason Grandy talked to me at all was in case I was still alive and thinking in there, but the reason vo told me stories about Flatworld in particular was because they—the doctors and everybody—did have some idea of what had happened to me. Not the Zyx part, not at first, but the fourth-dimension part. So Grandy was using a story about 3-D space being squashed down into 2-D space to help me understand how what was happening to me maybe had to do with 4-D space being squashed down into 3-D space.

The main character of Flatworld was a two-dimensional toad. His name was Tidy Teddy, 2-D Toad, which if you say it out loud is a good example of how geeky Grandy is about words, even just the sounds they make. Tidy Teddy wanted to go on a trip. You know, it's so long ago, I've lost the details. Zyx, can you remember that far back? Like, if I emptied my mind and let you take over my fingers, could you type one of Grandy's Tidy Teddy stories exactly the way vo told it? I could put in the capital letters and commas and stuff after.

yes

OK, go.

"As I told you before, dearheart, Tidy Teddy lived on one side of a giant tree, right by the trunk. One day he decided he wanted to go to the other side of the tree, because his friend Flibberty Florence the Floating Fly had told him how beautiful it was there, and he wanted to see for himself. Now, in our world that would have been as easy as snip snap snee, because he could've just hopped around the tree trunk, but in Flatworld he couldn't do that. Also, he couldn't tunnel under the tree or through the trunk the way the dreaded rock worms would, so the only choice he had left was to go over.

"Now, if you think about a tree, dearheart, there's the trunk and then the big branches and then the little branches and then the twigs and then the flowers and leaves, and if you tried to draw the outline of that tree on a piece of paper, it would take a very long line to wrap around the outside of every one of those branches and twigs and flowers and leaves. That line was the path that Tidy Teddy had to travel. What in our world would have been just a step or two became a quest in Flatworld. Who knows what adventures he might have on his journey? Who knows whom he might meet?"

OK, that's enough, thanks. It kinda hurts having you type like that.

Wow, snip snap snee. And the dreaded rock worms. I forgot about them. They could eat their way through anything. I used to have nightmares about them. Funny how strongly it comes back now, seeing the words again.

Maybe I should use the rock worms in Jarq. Hm. Now I have to figure out how I would draw them.

23 Days to Go

Rick is coming over for dinner. And how do you feel about that? the therapist said.

OK, I guess. Whatever.

Rick is Mom's new boyfriend. I think she really likes this one. He's not like that other stupid loud guy before. This one is quiet and nerdy. He brought her flowers once and he rubs her shoulders and stuff, and they get gooshy with each other. They think they're hiding it from us, but they're not. Gah. Truly squirmworthy.

felix like rick question mark

Oh, he's all right, I suppose, but with ZeroDay so close, I don't want to have to deal with him. As I mentioned, Mom says we need to keep on acting "normal," whatever that means, and in this case I guess she wants us to think it means things like having company over. But I think the real reason is she wants to sit with him out on the sunroom couch after dinner and cry on his shoulder.

why mom cry

Because she's scared. Because of ZeroDay coming, and how . . . how I might not survive. Gah, I don't want to talk about it. Going on.

The other thing that bugs me about Rick coming over is that we're going to have to keep telling the Story, which I hate, but we have to, because the Powers That Be (as Mom calls them, and she puts a world of snark into it) over at the Facility have made it clear that they don't want anyone to find out about Zyx and the Procedure. It's all Top Secret and Classified. Honestly, I don't know why we have to lie. Nobody would believe it anyway. But who knows what the Powers might do to us if we tell, so the Story it has to be.

Rick. Boyfriends. Mother Hubbard, I wish she would go back to having girlfriends again. They were nicer, mostly.

All right, fine, time for dinner with company.

e6 qxr exf check Stop it I'm trying *kd7 f8n check* Cut it out *kc7* I said cut it out!

chess fun zyx love chess chess fun

Yeah, I get that. Could you contain your enthusiasm, do you think, for a minute, so I can type?

. . .

Thank you.

And now that I have my fingers back, I can actually say: still twenty-three days to go.

Something freaky just happened. Rick brought his new tablet with him, and after dinner he says he wants to show me something, and I'm like, Oh no, he wants to *bond* with me, but then Mom gives me this "please go along" look, and Grandy (in Vera mode, it being Monday—with pearls) kicks my foot under the table, so I clear my throat and say, "Sure," and Rick shows me how he plays chess on the Internet. He has this app that signs into a server and there are all these games going on you can watch, or you can play. It's actually kinda cool. So he goes through the way all the different pieces move and how you win, and all of a sudden I start twitching like crazy. It's like convulsions, it's so intense, because Zyx is trying harder than I can remember since the early days to make my hands work.

kc8 nxq

Cut it out!

. . .

Thank you, again. OK. So Zyx gets my hands onto the tablet, my fingers start flying all over the place, tap tap tap, and I look down and I'm playing chess with someone. I mean, Zyx is, because I don't know what the hell is going on. Rick looks too and gets real still, and then a message pops up saying, "Black checkmated. KnightHawk67 wins." KnightHawk67 is Rick's screen name.

Then the message disappears because Zyx has started a new game. Vo makes the pieces jump a fraction of a second after the other person does, and the pauses while the other person thinks get longer, and in the pauses, Rick starts talking. "But I only just taught you the rules," he says, and, "Nobody plays this fast"—things like that. Another message pops up: "White resigns. KnightHawk67 wins."

Zyx immediately starts a third game, and Rick looks at the name on the screen and says in an awestruck voice, "This guy is an IM." "IM?" asks Grandy, and Rick says, "International Master." But it doesn't seem to make a difference to Zyx, who's moving just as fast as ever. At one point Rick says, "No, no, that's suicide," and then a second later, "Oh, wait, no, it's not . . ." Then he gapes at me and says, "How the heck did you see that? Nobody sees combos that fast. Nobody." Then the IM resigns.

chess pretty more chess

Yeah, I'm not so sure about that. Will you please shut up so I can type?

. . .

So anyway, a chat message pops up and the IM says, "It couldn't be more obvious that you're using a computer. I'm flagging your account." And then we can't play any more games, because the master has reported Rick for cheating.

Rick doesn't care. He asks if I've played chess before, and Mom says maybe somebody taught me the moves when I was little but basically no, and then Rick gets all worked up and says that I'm a phenomenon, a natural chess genius, a savant, blah blah blah.

Up until now, watching Zyx play, Mom has a couple of times started to say something and then stopped again, like she can't quite make up her mind if what is happening is good or bad. I can see how she might think it is bad, because, how to explain? But I have an idea. By now Zyx has let go enough for me to talk, so I mumble, "It's like my hands were moving by themselves."

Mom gives me a sharp look, but then the thinking line comes between her eyes and she nods, like, yeah, that'll work. "Well, you know," she says to Rick, "he suffered a traumatic brain injury when he was three." This is the Story, which Rick has heard, but now she adds the logical next bit: "So maybe there's a part of his mind that has this ability, but he's not really in touch with it except when he plays." Which is what I was thinking, so I'm glad she thinks it's smart. Now if someone asks me questions, it's OK if I can't answer them.

There's not much else to report after that. Rick was still excited and wanted to keep talking about it, but Mom firmly changed the subject, with some help from Grandy, and now I'm up in my room so I don't have to see through the sunroom window how the backs of their heads are getting closer together. Also, the next installment of Novaglyph—my absolute favorite web-comic ever—is due out tonight, and I want to check the rest of my regulars too. Zyx, have you calmed down?

chess pretty zyx love chess

You mentioned that.

22 Days to Go

There's something I haven't been saying, and I still don't want to say it, but I feel like if I don't I'm going to implode, so I'm making myself do it.

Type, Felix. Type!

OK, fine, typing.

The day before yesterday, when I wrote about Flatworld, there was a reason I didn't say anything about the day, which was that when I woke up, I couldn't move at all. My eyelids unglued themselves and breathing was OK, but other than that I was frozen. I pushed against the lockup and it just hurt, like trying to push through a concrete wall, so I stopped. Then I tried to go limp, to flop out of it, but that didn't work either.

After about five minutes Mom called me again, and then I heard her coming up the stairs and a big surge of adrenaline pumped through me and my whole body spasmed and then I was able to move again. When she stuck her head in and ordered me to get up, I pretended that the way I was twisting in the chair was wake-up stretching, and I didn't say anything about what had happened to anyone.

I don't want to die.

How can those words just sit there on the screen like that? I'm shaking so hard I can hardly type. I don't think I can go to school. I don't think I can do anything. I don't want to die.

not die

You can't say that. You don't know that.

explain

Yes, please, explain it to me.

. . .

Well?

not know how say

Well, then don't say. Sometimes I wish you would just shut up.

is three is one is not one is now is then is all now

I DON'T UNDERSTAND! LEAVE ME ALONE! LEAVE ME ALONE ALONE ALONE! IS THAT ENOUGH ALONES FOR YOU?

Zyx. Sorry.

no worries

What, you're all cool and laid-back now?

question mark

Never mind. Gah. Triple gah. I have to go to school. This sucks so deeply, I can't see the bottom of how deep the suckage is.

zyx love felix

Cut it out.

Still, thanks for saying. Breathing now.

OK. Sorry I freaked.

no worries

OK, that almost made me laugh. I swear you do have a sense
of humor, whatever you say. Let's go.

....

I felt better for a while after my freak-out this morning, but as
the day went on my body seemed to get heavier and heavier,
and I started to feel like the color was draining out of everything. By lunchtime a gray fog had come down over the world,
and each of my arms and legs felt like it weighed fifty pounds.
It was just so much work to do anything. To take a step. To
look up. To breathe.

Somehow I kept going, more or less. I ditched biology, but all
I did was sit behind the gym in a corner out of the wind and
look at the sunlight coming down through the bare branches.
Not like it seemed interesting to me at the time. It was just
where I pointed my eyes last before I stopped moving them.

sunlight through branches pretty

Not to me it wasn't.

light dance

What are you trying to do, spoil my bad mood?

question mark

Never mind. Forget it.

. . .

It did get a little better after I sat there for a while—only forty-pound weights on each arm and leg, and then only thirty—so I went back in and dragged myself through the rest of the afternoon. When I got home Mom and Grandy were off somewhere, and I said something stupid and mean to Bea and she went and practiced louder than usual, which got on my nerves the way I'm sure she meant it to, and then she made a point of sitting still and not looking at me when I went past to come upstairs, and may I just say that the whole day has been one long tunnel of gray horribleness? Gah.

zyx love felix

Yeah, yeah.

21 Days to Go

I talked to Hector today. I mean, he talked to . . . I mean, we talked.

Morning was unpleasant, because Tim the Bore finally launched his retaliatory strike or whatever. He came up behind me in the hall and threw a ball of chewed-up corn chips at the back of my head from about two feet away, and then while I'm standing there looking at it on my hands he follows up with some names—the R-word again of course, and fag, which is funny, because I really don't think he or anyone else has seen past Zyx to this other thing about me—and then he smacks the back of my head, just to make sure the corn and saliva mush gets nice and deep into my hair. Right then Mr. N comes around the corner with his whistle around his neck and a net bag of volleyballs in his hand and he doesn't even break stride, he takes Tim by the arm and steers him into the office, so I guess it's trouble time for Tim again. Jerk. He 100 percent deserves it.

I go into the bathroom to wash the mush out of my hair, as much as I can anyway, and then it's time for lunch. I'm sure I still smell like a soggy corn chip, so I don't sit with Barry and Mike and those guys like I sometimes do. Anyway, I'm tired of Mike bragging all the time about his Minecraft prowess. Instead I sit by myself, kinda sideways so I can look at the room if I want or just at the wall, and one of the times I'm looking at the wall and kerbopping the triangle, I feel the table bump and shake and I look around and Hector is sitting down. "Hi," he says. "OK if I sit with you?"

Me: Duuuuuuuuuhhhhhhhhhh . . . no, really, I don't say that, it's just what's happening in my brain. I can't speak, but somehow I manage to make my head move up and down. Doing the marionette thing again. Or, Zyx, was that you?

not

Uh-huh, I believe that. Maybe. So he sits and starts to eat, and I copy him so I won't be doing nothing, and then we're eating together, just him and me and the invisible awkward elephant

49

that has also joined us at the table. A year-long minute goes by, and then he says, "I saw Tim in the office, waiting to talk to Dr. A." Dr. A is our principal. "Did he do something else to you?"

"Yeah."

"What a loser."

"Yeah. But what can you do?"

"Yeah."

More lunch with the awkward elephant. I have no spit in my mouth, none at all, so chewing is, well, um, sticky and weird. Swallowing, too. All I can think of is corn chip corn chip corn chip, and I would say I wished I could die if I wasn't saying just yesterday that I don't want to die. Right when I'm ready to bolt, Hector points at my chest and says, "She's coming to MainahCon, you know."

I have no idea what he's talking about, so I look down and remember that I'm wearing my Novaglyph shirt, the one without words, just the symbol. I look back up at him, thinking, No way. Yes, it is the best webcomic in the universe, but nobody knows about it. Can he really actually know about it? Yes, he can, because he says, "Ash Cortez, who draws that. You know about MainahCon, right?"

"Yes. Of course. And seriously? Ash is going to be there?" Then for a second I'm not thinking about Hector even though he's right there, because, Ash. I could actually meet her. My comic-drawing hero. And MainahCon is just within the fifty-mile limit of the circle we're not supposed to go out of according to the Powers That Be, and it's the weekend after next so I'll still be alive.

"Yeah," he says. "She lives in Boston, didn't you know that? I wanna go meet her."

This makes me look fully at his face for the first time, and, Nelson, he's pretty. I like how his hair is so curly, with the clean, exactly shaped edge of it outlining his face, and he has such a pretty mouth, and his eyes are as brown as his face and they're doing that brain-eye-eye-brain thing, just like with Ms. C. I say something like, "Fwa?" and swallow and try again. "You follow Novaglyph?"

"Yeah."

"You draw?"

"Yeah." Mother Hubbard, could this boy be any more perfect? Somewhere in my brain a little voice is telling me to say, "Me too," but all I can do is gape at him.

He keeps looking back, and then he says, "Felix, can I ask you a personal question?"

"Fwa?" Great, Felix. But he gets it, because he goes ahead and asks: "What's wrong with you?"

That looks bad just to type it, but it wasn't. He wasn't being mean, and it wasn't the way people sometimes ask with this eager light in their eyes like they hope it's something unusual and dangerous so they can think, "Cool!" No, it was like he cares. But not even like, "Ooh, poor baby." Like a friend.

So, I know the drill. I'm supposed to tell him the Story. All of a sudden, though, I want to tell him the truth. I want to tell him everything, really badly. I even open my mouth to do it, but then Mom's face pops up on the screen of my mind, looking scared, and she's shaking her head and doing, "No, no," with her mouth—she's snarky about the Powers, but I get the feeling that underneath she's scared that if we tell, they might do something awful, like take me away—and my whole body jumps like a frog getting zapped. Zyx, was that you?

not

It must have been you. It was exactly how it always is when you're excited.

not not

By which you mean who knows what. Anyway, I'm flailing and flapping my mouth, and Hector starts to pull back. Not like I'm grossing him out, though. It's like he held out his hand and I slapped it. His eyes go away and his face closes up and he says, "Never mind, sorry I asked." Then he picks up his tray and starts to get up.

I really really want him to stay, so somehow in spite of the flailing I manage to say something like, "No! It's OK."

He stands there with his tray in his hands, looking at me. My face won't stop twitching, but my eyes stay on his eyes, and after a couple of seconds he sits back down.

"You're not going to blow up at me again?"

I shake my head, and he looks at me for another second and then says, "OK then." And he starts eating again.

I go back to eating too, and the awkward elephant comes back and joins us, because I haven't answered his question. I know Mom in My Mind is right, so it is going to have to be the Story, which I believe I have mentioned that I hate. Still, though, I think as I sit there, it does have little pieces of the truth in it, and I hear myself say, "I had an accident when I was three."

He keeps his head down, but I can tell he's listening, so I make myself go on. "And this accident, it left me with a traumatic brain injury."

He nods. Silence. Siiiiilence. Actually, though, I'm starting to get used to it. At last he says, "So that's why you . . ." and he does a move with his hand that means, all the weird things you do.

"Yeah."

"Oh." More silence. Then he says, "But you're still smart, right?"

For a second all I can do is stare at him. He stares back, and the same pulling-away look starts to come back into his face, so I say, a little louder than I mean to, "Yeah, I'm smart." A couple kids at the next table look over, but they look away again.

"Normal smart." Now he's almost whispering, because of the other kids.

I lower my voice too. "Yeah, normal. Whatever that means." Then he smiles for the first time. Only a little smile, but still, whammo.

"I thought so," he says. Yet more silence. Lunch is almost over. He finishes first and puts his hands on each side of his tray. Before he gets up, though, he says, "I know what it's like."

"You know what what's like?" I say, and then I think, Hey, that came out easy. Just like talking to Bea or Mom or Grandy.

"Having people think you're stupid, because you're not what they think of as normal." He wrinkles his nose—not quite a smile, but still—and adds, "Whatever that means," and I actually laugh. I never laugh at school. He goes on. "You know, 'cause of . . ." he says, and he does a move with his hand that means, his curly hair, the brown of his face.

I don't know what to say, so I just nod.

"So anyway, I just want to thank you," he says. "'Cause you're one of the only people at this school who ever really talks to me." Then he gets up and leaves, giving me one last look back as he goes.

What? I'M the only one who ever talks to HIM? What? What? I said, What?

20 Days to Go

We have just had another evening of chess fun with Rick. Usually he comes on Friday nights, but Saturday is the last dry run for the Procedure, which we have to leave for at some ridiculous hour of the morning, like four, so Mom set it up for him to come tonight instead. I could tell she was tense about it before he got here, though. I think he's been pushing her about the chess, and I guess she's still not sure how she feels about that.

At dinner Rick was acting in a way I haven't seen before, sticking his chin out and waving his fork around a lot when he talked, and when he looked at me it felt like his eyes had screwdrivers coming out of them, jabbing at me. I had to remind myself that all he knows is the Story. He doesn't understand that in twenty days I will either not be a chess player anymore or

I'll be dead, in which case I won't be a chess player anymore either, so, in twenty days I won't be a chess player anymore.

Mom tried to drop hints, mentioning my "surgery," which is the Story version of the Procedure, but I don't think he heard. A couple of times he talked right over her, and the second time he did it she sat back in her chair and looked at him like, Who *are* you?

Whatever. Zyx was making me jump all through dinner *chess pretty*

I was wondering how long it would take for you to speak up. Yeah, chess pretty. I'm starting to understand it a little myself, which is cool. Anyway, as soon as dinner is over, Rick pushes his dishes to one side and pulls out his tablet and says, "How 'bout it? Let's play some chess!" All fakey, you know, like a Little League coach or something. Serious eye-roll moment, but aside from knowing Zyx wants to play I'm getting more interested too, so as best I can—Zyx has me practically tied in knots—I go around and sit on the chair Rick has pulled out for me.

Next he explains that he has set up a new account with my name. Mom makes a concerned noise, and he says, "Don't worry, I paid for it," and she makes a concerned/protesting noise, and he says, "Oh, that. Don't worry—just his first name." He looks at me. "Actually, Felix was already taken, so I did Felix1, because you're going to be number one!" Over his shoulder Bea does a combo eye-roll and vomit-tongue, and the only thing that keeps me from laughing in his face is a straight look from Grandy under the bill of veir cap. Then I guess Rick gets the idea that he's coming on a bit strong, because he drops his eyes. "The password is chess4fun," he mumbles. "There has to be a numeral in it."

Bea asks to be excused and goes and starts practicing, and Grandy gets up and clears the table, paying attention as vo comes and goes. Mom sits and watches, sipping her wine. She's frowning, but interested too.

So we sign in to the site and the chessboard pops up, and Rick says, "You're a new player now, not me anymore, so nobody will have any way to tell who you might be or how strong you are. Do you understand?" I do a convulsion that is supposed to be a nod. "And sometimes really strong players create new accounts, so it won't automatically look like you're using a computer."

Mom says, "Did you get your account unfrozen?"

"No, they kicked me off the site. I had to start a new one." He sounds like he doesn't care even a little bit, so nobody says anything. "You're going to have to play some weaker players at first until your rating starts to go up, but that won't take long. Because you're so incredibly fast, I figure you should play bullet."

I can't speak, but fortunately Grandy steps in. "Bullet?"

"Yeah," says Rick. "One minute for each player for the whole game." Grandy raises veir eyebrows but says nothing.

Zyx must like this, because my hands leap onto the tablet by themselves *bullet fun but slow*

Slow, huh? Maybe you would like to play the whole game in one second?

more games that way

Riiiiight. Well, bullet is what we play, and once again the sense of Zyx driving my body is very strong. My hands get statue still, except when the fingers flick to tap out the moves. It's two taps for each move—the piece you're moving, and the square to move it to—and just like the first time, the games are mostly the other player thinking, so the rhythm goes taptap pause . . . other player moves taptap pause . . . other player moves taptap longer pause . . .

Once I figure out how to let go and let Zyx play, I am able to relax somewhat and glance up from time to time. The first time I do, Mom gives me a little question smile, and I nod back: Yeah, Mom, this is OK with me. If I could talk, I would say, Sometimes I can almost understand what's happening on the board.

Well, as expected, Zyx wins game after game. There are clocks on the screen, and ours always has at least fifty seconds left when the other player gets checkmated or resigns or runs out of time. Rick sits next to me, fidgeting and making noises, which would be distracting if it was actually me playing. He keeps saying things like "Ab-so-lute-ly incredible" and "I can't believe it."

We go on for about an hour without stopping. There's a way people can observe your games, with a counter so you can see how many, and by the end of the hour there are about a hundred people watching. There's a chat box too, and people are guessing who I am, and Rick says the names they are guessing are some of the top players in the world. Others are saying that

I have to be a computer, and then someone types, "Too fast even for a computer . . . It's God!" and then there are all these lols and laughy faces.

Um, Zyx, you're not God, are you?

god question mark

That's what I thought. But even if you're not THE God, mightn't you still be some kind of . . . You know what, never mind. I don't want to know. Sorry I asked.

. . .

By the end of the hour I'm starting to hurt, so I exchange another look with Mom, and she says, "This will be the last game." Rick looks like he's going to argue, but then maybe for the first time all evening he actually sees her face, so he closes his mouth again. Zyx wins one more game and then Rick signs us off and we all sit silent, with only Bea's music for sound. Then Rick says to Mom, "Margie, your son is a genius." Her name is Margo, as I've mentioned, but he calls her Margie. Gack.

Mom makes a little sound, like, Oh, really now . . .

"He is." He puts his hand on my shoulder, and I can feel it trembling. "The greatest natural chess genius the world has ever seen. He's going to be famous."

Mom's eyes dart back and forth like she's thinking of a whole bunch of different things to say and not saying any of them. Finally she says, "Yes, perhaps. Someday. If he wants."

Rick is back to not listening. "I know someone. A very strong player, a Grandmaster. She lives in Portland. Her name is Ursula Ots. She's from Estonia. I'd like to bring her to watch Felix play."

Now Mom's face looks chiseled out of granite. "I really don't think that's a good idea."

"She might be willing to coach him."

"We are done here."

Rick opens his mouth again, but Grandy cuts him off with a loud chair scrape that makes us all look. Vo stands up, putting down veir knitting. "This would be the sort of decision that needs to be slept on," vo says in a voice that I can hear is stagey but Rick probably can't. "Right now it's time for chores. Felix, get to it. Lickety-split." I jump up, or lurch up anyway, and figure out something to pick up and carry into the kitchen to look busy, and the discussion is over.

So, maybe this Ursula person will come. That could be interesting.

chess pretty

You mentioned that. I have to do my homework now.

19 Days to Go

The only thing I have to report about today is that it has been less fun than usual for a Friday because tomorrow, all day, is the trip to the Facility to finish the Fitting of the Apparatus. Gah, all these Capital Letters. But, that's how it feels, so, Whatever. The Facility is the science complex where the accident happened and where the Procedure is going to be performed. It's a long way from here, back where we used to live. (Of course the fifty-mile rule doesn't apply to driving there.) And may I just say I am not looking forward to any part of this, at all?

Anyway, since we're returning to where it all started, I thought I would do some more backstory.

After the accident, when I was paralyzed, Mom says they

couldn't get any response from me at all, so at first they thought that my brain had been damaged. Not just damaged—destroyed. They thought I was brain-dead. (That was no fun to type.) I wasn't, though. My brain was working same as always. Zyx, I know you remember that time, because you remember everything.

not remember know be

What was it like for you?

not dance more

By which you mean who knows what.

. . .

Fine. Anyway, the kind of paralyzed I was was the rigid carved-in-stone kind, not limp, and of course I was paralyzed in the Pose, so they had me strung up with a bunch of those pulley-and-weight things. I've seen a picture. All I could do besides just hang there was breathe and blink, and it was a slow, slow, heavy blink, cllllooooooooose, and then ooooooooopen, like a steamroller rolling back and forth. Of course my heart was still beating too, but otherwise I couldn't even twitch a finger.

I could hear and understand everything that people were saying when they were in the room, though. Sometimes that was incredibly frustrating, but sometimes it was kinda cool.

Frustrating was Mom and Bea sitting by my bed and crying and me feeling really really lonely and scared and wanting Mom to hold me but not being able to say anything or reach my arms toward her.

Cool was watching and listening to the doctors and nurses and getting ideas about what kinds of people they were. There was one nurse who would look into my eyes like she was really looking at me, and she would talk to me. It's going to be all right, Felix, she would say. Everything is going to be fine, sweetie. And she would put her hand on my forehead and smooth my hair. It was so nice.

And there was this one doctor who was talking to another doctor once, a man doctor and a woman doctor. They were standing at the foot of the bed, right where my dead glass zombie eyes were staring at them, but they didn't know I could see them with my dead glass zombie eyes, and man doctor kinda looks around, and then he hooks a thumb at me in the bed and says, "Zucchini."

Woman doctor makes a little noise that could mean anything, and man doctor goes on in the same jokey braggy voice, "Hopeless case. Yoon and Perkins think there's a chance of recovery, but I know a persistent vegetative state when I see one." Which shows what he knew, I guess.

Perkins? Yeah, I think that's right. Wow, it really comes back when you write it. Zyx, are you helping me remember?

no

But it was Perkins, right?

yes

So I remembered myself. Cool. Aaaaand Mom just called lights-out. Early bedtime because of tomorrow morning. Four a.m. Such a time should not exist, and I definitely shouldn't have to get up into it. I am tired, though. I wasn't quite completely locked up this morning, but wow, did I have to push to get moving, and my body hurt all day. So I guess I could sleep. Good night, Zyx.

good night

Sweet dreams, don't let the bedbugs bite.

question mark

Never mind. Good night.

zyx love felix

Sure. Thanks.

18 Days to Go

So the Fitting happened, and we're home again. Besides that, though, something else happened that I'm not sure I'll be able to explain . . . but maybe I should just let it come into the telling when it comes.

When Mom rousted me out of my chair, it was still completely dark. I growled at her, but she kept shaking me until I broke through the creaky-pain-freeze and stumbled around getting dressed, and then stumbled out to the car. It was just me and Mom and Bea—Grandy stayed home. I chose the backseat, and as soon as Mom started driving I put my player on shuffle and scooched down as far as it seemed like she would let me. She gets freaky about seat belts across stomachs, as opposed to "low and tight across your lap," because, I suppose, if we were in an accident I would get sliced in half right back to my spine, which now that I think about it, yuck, so I guess she has a point.

Anyway, she didn't seem to be paying any attention, so I got my head down below the bottom of the window and just kinda dozed off and on, watching during the eyes-open times as the sky got lighter. Random things went flitting by in the part of the sky I could see: telephone poles, traffic-light poles, buildings and signs and trees. They had no rhythm. Flick, flick, flickflick . . . empty stretch . . . big building zooms by . . . little empty bit . . . flickity-flick . . . never repeating. And it was cool how my tunes were going beat, beat, beat, against this other randomness.

music beat music free rhythm between sing dance

Um, sure, you could say that. Anyway, it was one of the first really not-cold mornings of spring, and in the breeze from Mom's cracked-open window I zoned out and managed to let worry be somewhere else for a little while. So, good.

The sun was halfway up the sky by the time we got to the Facility, and they were expecting us. The guard waved us through. I got the same squirt of adrenaline I always get looking at the concrete buildings and the fences and all the power pylons, and the worry came back. Bea glanced back at me, and I could see the worry in her face too.

When we parked, Dr. Yoon and Dr. Gordon were there to meet us, and as always I had to keep myself from laughing at the size difference between them. Dr. Yoon is so small, and Dr. Gordon is so huge. Beyond that, Dr. Yoon is like somebody's cheerful bustling mom, but with shrewd eyes watching you all the time too, and Dr. Gordon is this big lumbering mumbling man who never looks anyone in the face. When he talks, which isn't much, he talks to his shoes, except when he's working on the Apparatus, when he acts like the world's largest twelve-year-old science nerd. Dr. Yoon is a medical doctor, and Dr. Gordon is a PhD doctor.

After hi hi hi all around, the two doctors led us down the spiral stair into the cubical chamber where the Apparatus is. There are cables and hoses everywhere, and in the walls there are huge fans for sucking the air out and then pumping it back in again, because, I forgot to mention, the ZeroMoment needs to happen in as close to a total vacuum as possible.

The Apparatus itself looks like a giant twenty-seventh-century robot baseball. There's a hatch that opens, and inside there are a bunch of armatures that together make up a skintight

Felix-shaped total-body cast. I have a mask for breathing, and the armatures fit so close that I cannot move at all. For this to work, we have to re-create the Pose exactly, and how we will know we have it exactly is, Zyx will tell us. Vo can feel when we are microscopically farther away from or closer to the precise position, so they've installed two halves of a keyboard, one for each hand, under the fingers at the end of each arm-armature. Once they close the hatch, all I can do is wait while they use enormous machines to twiddle my left little toe up a half a millimeter and then down again, based on what Zyx types.

almost dance

You mean, when the position is exactly right?

yes almost dance

But not quite.

. . .

Still, it must feel good. I don't know about you, but even though I am scared out of my mind about this, I would sure love to be able to move any way I want.

. . .

Do you even move, where you live?

dance dance dance

Which doesn't exactly answer my question. Whatever. I'll tell
you something though: if this does work, one of the very first
things I am going to do is stretch. I'm going to stretch myself
into the exact opposite shape of the Pose, hands way up high,
feet way down low, back arched back . . . oh, Mother Hubbard,
I bet it is going to feel incredible.

Anyway, back to the Apparatus. Let's see—what did I leave
out? Well, did I mention I'm naked for this? And smeared
with slippery goop? And, not yet, but on the day, every hair on
my entire body shaved off?

And there's one other thing, not for practice, but on ZeroDay:
they are going to stop my heart right before the ZeroMoment
and then restart it right after. They say it's because I have to
be absolutely still. Mom doesn't like the heart-stopping part
one bit, and now that I mention it, neither do I. I still laugh,
though, when I think of the time Dr. Yoon said about the
ZeroMoment, "You won't feel a thing," and Bea and I had a

look go between us that was the same as both of us saying, "Because you'll be DEAD!"

So on ZeroDay they'll seal the chamber, and the electricity will build—it is going to take an astronomical number of volts—and the fans will suck all the air out of the room, and they'll zap me to stop my heart, and then the Apparatus will do its inter-dimensional membrane reopening thing or whatever, which they think should take just a gazillionth of a second, and then, whoosh, the air gets pumped back in and the machine zaps me again to restart my heart, and a medical team comes running in case the heart-starting zap doesn't work, and the Apparatus pops open and there I am, either separate or still fused, and either alive or dead. Of course we're all hoping for separate and alive.

That's how it's supposed to go on the day. Yesterday was sim-pler. I peed one last time and then stripped down and gooped up, and then Dr. Yoon helped me climb up the long laddery steps. She wore plastic gloves that went all the way up over her elbows, to be able to grip my arm, she said, but also no doubt to keep the goop off herself. She's such a tidy person, with such tidy clothes. Then she and this other technician/nurse person helped me lower myself into the Apparatus. It wasn't quite as totally embarrassing as it could have been, being naked and slippery, because they were being so Scientific. It was a fiddly business, though, with bonks and pinches, and it took a long time because we were trying not to get goop everywhere.

Once I was finally in, though, I felt the same thing I have felt every other time, which is that the armatures fit so close that there's no pressure anywhere. It's like being weightless. All you can do is let go and float. I get kinda dreamy sometimes. I wouldn't call it sleeping exactly, but my mind goes wandering off to the oddest places.

This time, at first, I'm tense and uncomfortable. I have an itch on my leg that there is no way to scratch—I can't even wiggle it against something—so for a little while that bugs me. But then the floating feeling takes over and my mind begins to float too, more than I can ever remember before, and then I have this strange experience, or maybe vision is the right word? I'm not sure. Whatever it was, it was intense, so I want to try to describe it.

First I start thinking about how my body is totally encased by the Apparatus, right at the skin level, and then how the Apparatus is encased in the air around it, atom to atom, and then how the air in the cubical chamber is encased in the walls, which are thick metal and concrete.

Then I think about how if you were made of neutrinos and could pass through the walls, you would come to solid rock except in the straight-up direction, where you would break through quickly to the air of the atmosphere, but sideways and especially down there is the rock of the planet, and how if you went down far enough, you would get to where the rock is molten and swirling.

Then I zoom out even more so I can see the whole sphere of the planet, ginormous, with the tiny cube of the chamber hollowed out right under the surface in one place, and inside that the sphere of the Apparatus, and inside that the exact human shape of me.

Then I go swooping down inside myself and think about skin and muscles and bones and then the cells they are made of and then all the bits and pieces inside the cells, the DNA and whatever, and then I zoom in on one DNA molecule until I'm focusing on its single atoms, and then protons and neutrons and electrons (and hey, school turns out to be good for something—it gives you names for the parts of your hallucinations).

I don't know anything about subatomic particles except having heard that they exist, so then, like a roller coaster hitting the bottom of a big hill and swooping up again, I go flying all the way back out, atoms molecules cells body Apparatus air chamber planet, and then on, atmosphere, space, more space, huge vast limitless expanses of space, other planets sun stars galaxies all whipping by until I can't think any bigger. What's past the biggest you can think?

And then swooping back in again, even faster, one long incredible fall through the human-shape of me and this time down past where I don't know how to go any smaller and I find myself somehow looping around to out-past-too-big again, so that everything seems to fit inside the smallest place inside me and vice versa. And then for a while I'm not sure if I'm inside the universe or the universe is inside me. The only thing that seems for sure is that somewhere in all the dancing around of whatever it is that dances, there's the human-shape of me, with either everything inside of it or it inside of everything, or somehow—don't ask me how—both at the same time. Then I feel a hand touching my face and hear Dr. Yoon's voice saying, "Felix, wake up."

yes now felix see something

I thought I would hear from you. Well, I guess I did, but I don't see what I saw, if you see what I mean.

saw dance felt dance felix dance

To which I respond, hm.

. . .

Yeah, I don't know what else to say about it either. Just that it was intense.

Anyway, once the Fitting was done, it was time to get cleaned up and have some food and go home. Food was this awkward crappy meal sitting at a table in a little kitchen sort of place. Mom had her lips pressed shut and that tense line between her eyes, and Bea was listening to her headphones with her eyes closed, which left me still feeling trippy and elsewhere, Dr. Gordon staring down at his sandwich, and Dr. Yoon not being able to get any of us to talk. Everyone was quiet on the drive home, too, and as soon as we got home we all went to our separate places in the house. It's not much of a house—just another modest bungalow in the faceless suburbia of the world—but at least it's big enough for each of us to have a separate place. Thank goodness for that.

I keep thinking about that swoopy dreamy time, how there was inside me and outside me and the me-shaped boundary between the two, and now that's mixed up in my head with Bea's sinfonia, the middle voice . . . the threeness of things . . . it's all very strange, but my brain can't seem to leave it alone. That said, it has gotten way late and I am completely exhausted. Sleep.

17 Days to Go

One of the things that happens when you have a piano-genius sister is you have to go to all these concerts. Bea plays piano for everything at her school: choir, the spring musical, jazz band, singers and violinists, anyone who needs an accompanist. And then there are her own recitals too. I don't mind most of the time. I like the music. The part that's less fun is when Zyx gets excited and I start flailing in my seat. The people around me hold their heads forward so carefully, and it's like they're shouting, I'm not looking at you, I'm not looking at you, see how nonchalantly I'm not looking at you? It's way worse than if they just looked. But, whatever. I'm used to it, mostly, I guess.

So that's what today was about, an afternoon concert at Littlefield High. When we arrived Bea peeled off in the direction of the beeps and blats of people warming up in the band room, and Mom and Grandy and I (Grandy with purse and clunky jewelry, it being Sunday) continued on into the auditorium.

As soon as we step inside the doors I see the back of Hector's head, and immediately I want the exactly opposite things of sitting right next to him and staying as far away from him as possible. It's not up to me, though, because Grandy is in the lead and picks seats right inside the door, halfway across the auditorium from Hector. From where we are sitting, all I can do is watch him move his head. He turns it to the left a lot to talk to the woman sitting next to him, so I figure she must be his mom—Mrs. Dandicat. (Yes, of course I know his last name.) She has freckles and rusty-red hair. Hector also talks with the man sitting past her, who I figure must be his dad. He's tall and handsome, and his face is even darker than Hector's.

Kids with instruments start coming out onto the stage and then the lights go down and the music starts, but I can't tell you much about it, because aside from thinking about all the people being so careful not to look at me, my brain all of a sudden gets an idea. We have a plan for Grandy to take me and Bea to MainahCon, and what occurs to me is, would Hector maybe possibly like to join us?

After the concert our two families leave in opposite directions, so it looks like there's no chance of such a question being asked today, but I'm wrong about that, because we have a family tradition that after concerts Bea gets ice cream to celebrate. It's always at this little corner shop on one end of the main street downtown. It has old wooden ice cream signs with the paint peeling off, a random kite hanging from the ceiling, steamed-up windows, and this sweet rich smell like the air is made of sugar. Inside, what with the big drink machine humming in one corner and the tableful of high school girls yakking in another, there is room for us and one other family, and the other family, ahead of us in line, is the Dandicats again. All four Dandicats, because Hector's brother plays trombone in the jazz band. And of course Bea is with us now too, so we make quite a crowd.

As soon as my mom and Hector's mom see each other, they say hello and start chatting. Apparently they know each other a little, from volunteering at the library, by their talk. Great. Just what I need. Then the moms are saying everyone's names, and Hector does the tiniest eye-roll when he nods after his name, like, how funny that nobody knows we already know each other, which in spite of the monster awkwardness almost makes me laugh. When Hector's dad talks he has an accent, and Mom remarks on it and then she's talking French with him and he smiles for the first time and my heart goes flip because his smile looks like Hector's smile.

While the French is going on, I try to get my face to lift up to the position that a person's face would usually be in if that person was maybe going to ask someone else a question, but it stays stubbornly down until the French stops, and that happens because Bea suddenly points at Hector's shirt and says, "Hey, Morning Hill." So I look, and sure enough, he's wearing a podcast fandom shirt. I don't listen to Morning Hill, but Bea loves it.

Hector's face lights up and he starts to answer, but then it's his turn to tell the ice cream person what he wants. He orders a pistachio cone. Bea gets him talking again after, though, so then the Dandicats are standing and listening to the two of them geek out about their favorite podcast while our family orders, and I still can't speak. Then just when the ice cream person asks me for my order, Hector tells Bea that he's going to MainahCon, so then I can't think of anything to ask the ice cream person for but pistachio, because Hector asked for it, even though I've never had it before.

So now for a second it seems like everything is going to be OK, because I found out he's going even if I couldn't make myself ask, but then the ice cream person hands me my cone and I take too big a first bite and then practically collapse onto the floor from a combination of brain freeze and Zyx freaking out about the flavor. It's been a long time since you've done that.

zyx love pistachio

You think I don't know that? But I'd forgotten how excited you could get about new flavors. It was like the old days, right after the accident. Sometimes I sure do wish you could figure out how to tone it down.

question mark

You made it look like I was having a seizure. And before I could even stand up straight again they were leaving, and the ice cream fell out of my cone, and Hector gave me a look like I was pitiful and ridiculous.

not

Oh, all of a sudden you're an expert on human facial expressions? That's a laugh.

not

Oh, shut up. Whatever you mean. But at least now I know he's going to the con. So maybe I'll see him there. Even if he has decided that I'm a freak after all. Gah.

16 Days to Go

I saw Hector again at school today, in the library, and we talked, and . . . and, I have no idea what is going on. I guess he wants to be friends, but beyond that does he . . . I mean, is he . . . and, what are these three dots things called, again?

ellipses

Yes . . . that's . . . right . . . thanks . . . ellipses. Like the egg-shaped things that are not . . . quite . . . circles. Cool. And, yeah, I'm totally avoiding saying the next thing about Hector. But, honesty in writing—that's another thing from today, from talking again to Ms. C, which I should tell about too. And maybe I should just describe from the beginning again. OK, doing that.

I didn't get a lot of sleep, which meant that even though lock-up wasn't quite as bad as usual, it was still unpleasant waking up. Lights seemed too bright and voices seemed too loud, and it lasted into school, so in study hall I took the option to go to the library. I was thinking that I would sit in one of the carrels at the back and rest, but as soon as I walked through the door I saw Hector at the table over by the window, and he glanced up and saw me too. He didn't exactly jump up and wave, but I don't think he's that kind of person. He just tilted his head and looked at me. Zyx seemed far down inside, the way vo is sometimes . . . Zyx, are you there?

yes am there

Oh, good. Doing OK?

question mark

Never mind. Just checking. Anyway, Zyx was deep, so I was able to hold still and look back, and after a second he made a motion with his head like, What do you suppose would happen if you came over here and sat down? In my mind I balanced embarrassment about the ice cream incident against wanting to suggest meeting at the con. Wanting to suggest won, so I went over. Zyx, help with words again?

yes

Thanks.

Hector: "Hi."

Me: "Hi."

Silence.

Well, that was simple. No need for help remembering there. But we did speak again. Or he did, because my brain was going wanga wanga wanga and I couldn't make my mouth work. "You OK?"

The way he asks it, I hear in his voice the same thing I heard when he asked me what's wrong with me, which is that he really cares, and that surprises me because I was so sure about the "Omigod, what a freak" look, but maybe not after all, so I say, "Yeah, thanks. Worst brain freeze ever"—which is only a little lie—"but I'm fine."

He nods, and it seems like we're done with that. More silence. His face doesn't say shut up even a little, though, so then to my own surprise I say, "Do you ever get the feeling like your head is full of dark clouds?"

"I guess, maybe. You mean, like, sad?"

"Um, sorta. Sad with a side of doom."

Then an amazing thing happens: he laughs. He does it quietly, because we're in the library, but it's such a wonderful sound, and I love the way the corners of his eyes get a little spray of wrinkles around them when he does it. I just love looking at him and listening to him and being with him, you know?

yes know

Gah. That was, whadayacall, a rhetorical question.

question mark

Never mind. Just keep quiet, will you?

. . .

Thank you. Going on now. What's next is Hector says, "Do you feel that way now?"

"Yeah, some. Kinda medium. Not as bad as sometimes."

"How come?"

And there I am again, wanting really badly to tell him everything. In about two seconds I whip through the same routine as before: the Story, which I hate, the Powers, can't tell, and then again also the realization that the Story is better than nothing, because it does have parts of the truth in it. A big scary thing is going to happen soon. I can say that much at least.

While I'm taking my two seconds I see his face doing the pulling-away thing again, and again he says, "Never mind, sorry I asked," but this time I handle it better.

"No, it's OK," I say. "It's just that, um . . . not many people know." He waits for me to go on, so I tell him the rest of the Story. "You know about the traumatic brain injury." He nods. "Well, now I have . . . it caused a tumor in my brain." Saying the lie makes me squirm, but I keep going. "And, they say . . . they have to . . . well, anyway, in a few weeks I have to go . . ." I wave my hand. My body is shaking.

His face changes again and, wouldn't you know, another look I love. What's the word? Compassion. "Surgery?" he says.

"The Procedure," I say, and getting to say it makes my voice crack.

He makes a move with his hand like reaching out to touch me, but then stops. "Are they going to . . ." he says, and with his fingertip he makes a slicing motion in the air over his forehead.

"Uh, something like that. It's complicated."

"Whoa." He looks away for a second, I guess imagining the scene. He looks back. "Is it going to hurt?"

I shrug.

"Are you scared?"

"What do you think?" I say, which is weird, because usually I'm only sarcastic at home. The skin over his eyes furrows up and his chin goes hard, and, Nelson, I seem to love everything about this boy's face. "Sorry," I say, before he can say anything. "Yeah, I'm scared. I'm scared to death." Saying it like that I can feel how true it is, and I duck my head, because my throat has squeezed shut and my eyes have gone swimmy.

This time he does touch me, just a hand on the sleeve of my shirt for a second, touch and gone. "Well, that sucks," he says, and the tone of his voice is no more than like, Shoot, we missed the bus, and I look up, and now he's doing this one-eyebrow-raised thing like, I see your sarcasm and raise you one. Then I laugh, and one tear squirts out of each eye, and he smiles, and his nose does this crinkly thing that, gah, I'm getting boring on the subject.

you love

Yeah, but I'm going to stop mentioning each thing. Let's just say I think he's totally beautiful, OK?

ok

Rhetorical . . . oh, never mind. ANYWAY. Right at the tear-squirt moment I really REALLY want to be talking about ANYTHING else, so I open my mouth without any idea what I am going to say, and what I say is, "I want to ask you something." I do?

We have gotten pretty close to each other, bending in a little to keep our talk quiet, but now he leans back and moves one arm in front of him. "OK?" he says.

The con, the con, goes part of my brain, but what comes out is something else I realize I have been wondering: "What did you mean when you said the other day that I'm the only one who talks to you?"

He shakes his head. "Not the only one," he says. "One of the only ones."

"You have a ton of friends, I thought."

"Yeah, you know, people I hang out with, but I wouldn't call most of them friends. People I hang out with and people who really know me—not the same."

"So just a few."

"Yeah. Annabel and Markus, they're cool. It's, like, so easy being with them, you know they are there because they really wanna be. You can tell they like you for who you are."

"Do you like them too?"

"Well, yeah. I like them fine. I like lots of people. I'm gregarious." What a great word. Mother Hubbard, I love this boy.

"But the others?"

"Oh, they're all right, y'know, they're fine. But when they talk to me, there's always this distance, this sorta careful separation. And every once in a while someone'll get weird about how they say the word 'black,' like they think they're not allowed to use it or something, and it gets all awkward. And once or twice I've even gotten the N word." He falls silent. I think to myself that I've heard people call him other names too, I guess because he does seem kinda girlish sometimes, but maybe it's like with the way Zyx makes me—maybe mostly they can't see past the first thing. But I don't say anything out loud.

When Hector goes on, his face is serious. "Here's what bugs me. 'Cause, you saw, my dad is from Haiti, but my mom is American—she's white. And growing up, I always thought of myself as a white boy, just like everyone I went to school with. But to most everyone around here, I'm the black kid. And then when we go down to Boston to visit my dad's people, I'm the white kid again. It's like I'm stuck between two worlds."

I stare at him, because pinball lights are flashing in my head. The threeness of things, the middle voice, me and Zyx . . . it all fits together. I repeat like a robot, "Stuck between two worlds."

"Yeah."

I can't help it—it just comes out by itself. "I know *exactly* what you mean," I say. Fervently, that's the word for how I say it.

He doesn't say anything, but he gives me a look like, Oh yeah, how could you possibly? See, I forgot he doesn't know about Zyx. So then I start flapping my hands and stuttering, but I manage to say something about how I'm not brain-damaged, so I don't belong in the world of people with disabilities, but people think I am, so I also don't belong in the world of people without disabilities. And he purses his lips and nods, like, All right, I'll allow that. The thing about people who show their doubt, when you convince them, you can tell. Cool.

The rest of the talk is not important—stuff about people we both know. Gossip, I guess. But the way we're talking now, there's a no-worries rhythm. Like, we're friends. I get distracted a couple of times because I keep noticing this cinnamon smell in the air which I wonder if it is coming from his hair, but I just get my mind back on listening and pick up the thread again. And then there's the part right at the end when it's time to go and once again the words come out of my mouth by themselves: "So see you at the con maybe," and he nods and says, "Yeah, maybe see you there." So, good.

And the other thing, with Ms. C. On the way out after last

bell I bump into her again, and she asks to talk to me and steers me into an empty classroom, and then she asks me whether I've decided to enter the writing contest. I feel shy all of a sudden, but the look on her face is so open and nice, I say, "Well, yeah, maybe, I've had this idea," and she smiles and nods, so I talk some about the threeness of things, about the sinfonia and Hector and about being between two worlds myself, and her smile gets this extra twist and she says, "That sounds wonderful, Felix. You should write it all down. It's really good." So then I feel all warm and can't talk for a second, and she goes on, "But, you don't have much time. The deadline is Friday."

"This Friday?"

"Yes, this Friday. But that's enough time. And if you can get it done by Thursday, I'll look at it and make suggestions, if you like. Another pair of eyes always helps."

I feel confused by that, and say, "But . . ."

"Don't worry," she says. "It will still be all your writing. Editors, good editors anyway, don't take over or write for you. They tell you what they like and make suggestions, and then you can change it or not, as you see fit."

"Oh. Well, OK, I'll try. Thursday."

"Thursday. And, Felix, one more thing."

"Yeah?"

"I told you before that I like your voice, and one reason is your eye for detail. Another reason is, I think you are an honest writer. That's also really important. The more honest your writing is—the more you say exactly what you think and feel—the better it will be. Remember that."

"Honest."

"Yes."

"OK," I say, and then I have to run to catch the bus.

And now my head is full of stuff I want to write about the threeness of things, so I'm going to stop writing this and start working on that instead. And maybe Ash has posted by now too. I can't believe I'm going to maybe meet her in a few days. Should I take some Jarq drawings to show her? I could. But would I die if she didn't like them? Yes, I would. So probably, no, I won't.

15 Days to Go

Wow, I just learned something big about our family. I'm not sure how I feel about it. It's weird. And she doesn't show stuff like this usually, but I think Bea is really freaked out. I want to go talk to her, but right now she's in her room with the door closed, being left alone like she asked.

But, first things first. Last night when I was working on my threeness paper, Mom came and leaned in the doorway the way she does when she wants to talk medium serious and asked me about chess. She said Rick had asked her again about bringing the Estonian Grandmaster over to see Zyx play. I could tell by the way she asked that she was still irritated with Rick, but she also said that seeing as how in a few weeks Zyx would be gone (being careful just to mention that one possible scenario), if it was truly interesting to me, she figured I might get to meet some people and see some things I wouldn't otherwise get to meet or see, so go ahead if you want. And I said, "Sure, let's go ahead," and Zyx made me twitch the way vo does when vo's happy *chess pretty*

You don't mind at all saying the same thing over and over, do you?

not mind chess pretty

I rest my case. So now on Friday Rick is bringing this Ursula Ots person over after dinner to play some chess. Should be interesting. I'm glad it's on Friday, because I will have turned in my threeness paper by then.

After that, sleep, wake, breakfast, bus, school. Nothing much to report. I was on the lookout for Hector, but the two times I saw him, there were other people around and basically I froze up, so we didn't talk. I wonder . . . I wonder if . . . Wow, I can't even type it.

I wonder if he likes boys too.

There, I did it.

many like many hector like many

Sure, lots of people like lots of people, but I mean *like* like.

like like question mark

Yeah, like like, like, you know, more than friends like. Like, want to get closer like. But, with the Procedure coming up, it seems wrong . . . but what if . . . I mean . . . what if this is my only chance . . . triple-quadruple gah! Why does this have to be so hard?

. . .

Uh-huh. ANYWAY. So then home, and another family dinner. Mom and her evil plans. It really does make us talk to each other, eating together.

Which is what I've been trying to get to. Conversation got around to school, and I started looking for an opening to bring up my paper. I was actually nervous about it, because I wanted to ask them all about their threenesses, you know, like, in what way might *you* be the middle voice between two other voices? And, this is stupid, because they are my family, but I thought . . . well, I just felt like they might laugh at my idea. But I did it anyway, and they didn't laugh. I asked Grandy first, because vo's always talking about stuff like this—Ideas, Philosophy, Big Concepts about Life and Stuff. Also, I figured I knew what vo'd say. Vo was in Vera mode again, btw, with a skirt and bracelets and big dangly earrings, but I'm still going to use vo and ven, because vo always corrects me if I use either she or he.

Of course the first thing vo says is, "I suppose you know what I'm going to say."

"The Vera/Vern thing."

"Well, yes, dearheart, naturally. It is rather a tidy and complete model of the idea you are exploring, wouldn't you agree?" When Grandy is Vera, vo talks more like one of Mom's British mysteries than when vo's Vern.

"What is your original ends-with-X name, anyway?" I ask. "If you have one?" This question is sort of a joke, because I've asked it about a hundred times, and vo never answers. Vo likes to have veir secrets. Like Dad's other parent. He had two parents, of course, but all I know about the other one is that vo died, or maybe disappeared, and nobody will tell me anything about ven, even a name. It's like there's a family rule about not talking about it.

Grandy gets an annoying little smile on veir face—smirk is the word for that smile—and says, "Now, dearheart, you know I can't tell you that."

Usually that's the end, but this time I ask the next question, because, the paper. "Why not?"

"Oh, well, you know, if I did have such a name—note I'm not saying whether I do or not—nothing frightful would happen if I told you. But it has become important to me that no one around me who doesn't already know my birth name learn it, whether or not it ends with X."

"Why?"

"Because then someone might assume vo knew which biological sex I was at birth, and then vo might decide that one of Vera or Vern was the real me and the other was only an act, or a joke, or worse, a mental illness, which is most certainly not the case. I am Vera, and I am Vern, and I am also both and neither." Thanks, Zyx, for the word for word.

welcome

I'm going to have to learn to take notes or something if . . . when, I mean . . . gah, going on. "Both? Neither?"

"Both, because both come completely naturally to me. Neither, because the place they come from is a sort of middle me, where I don't believe I actually have a gender. The me I am when I'm by myself on the seventh day each week."

"Door locked, not talking, not eating, not wearing any clothes."

"That's right, pet." I hate it when vo calls me pet, but whatever. And of course I know better than to ask what I would see if I walked in on ven naked.

Next I turn to Bea, who is playing piano on the table, as usual. "Hey." Nope. "Hey."

She does this slow returning-from-a-million-miles-away thing, which is her in a nutshell. "What?" she says.

"Threenesses. Got one? Are you an end point, or in the middle? All that stuff." She stares at me blankly—typical Bea—but then she seems to get an idea and opens her mouth to say something. She doesn't get to speak, though, because all of a sudden Mom makes this odd sound, a kind of bigger than usual hiccup, and gets up so quickly her chair nearly tips over, and runs out of the room. "I can't, I can't," she's crying as she runs up the stairs, and then, "Not another one." Her door closes, click not slam. Bea and I sit there with our mouths open. Grandy gets up, looking serious, and says, "Don't worry, children, I'll take care of this. Go ahead and keep eating," and goes upstairs after Mom.

14 Days to Go

So last night I was writing about the big family secret, but then Mom called me back downstairs to talk some more, and I meant to come back and finish but I never did. Another cliffhanger. Ha. Next time I'm doing it on purpose. Turns out one thing writing seems to be about is torturing the reader as much as possible. Weird, but cool.

Picking up from Grandy going upstairs after Mom, the next thing that happens is Bea looks at me and says, "I hate it when she freaks."

"Yeah."

"What do you think is wrong?"

"I have no idea. Stress, I guess. You know."

We sit. Bea pokes her macaroni around on her plate with her fork. "This Rick person," she says. "I don't like him very much."

"Yeah, me neither. He's gotten weird about the chess."

"Are you really going to do that?"

"Sure, why not? Zyx likes it." We look each other in the eyes. "Kind of a going-away present, know what I mean?"

She nods. Then she gets up and goes into the living room and starts playing the piano. My stomach has knotted up the way it tends to do when Mom is upset, but I also remember that before dinner I was hungry, so I sit there making my teeth chomp and my tongue push the food around and my throat swallow. Then Grandy is back with Mom standing behind ven, her face all blotchy from crying. She says, "Felix, please come into the living room. We need to have a Talk."

Gah. I hate Talks with a capital T.

Mom has to put her hand on Bea's shoulder to get her to stop playing. Then she sits on the edge of the big stuffed chair, hugging herself with one arm. I stay standing in the archway back into the dining room.

"Children," Mom says. "Beatrix. Felix. I have something to tell you." She looks down into her lap, then up again. "I am sorry to bring this up at this time. Your dad and I could never agree about telling you, and after he . . . after the accident, it went clean out of my head for a long time, and then it became a thing that had happened a long time ago, before other things started taking up all the family's attention. So when I thought of it, I never felt it was the right time for . . . for this bit of family history." I glance at Bea and see the same look of suspense on her face I figure is on mine. Grandy is scanning from face to face, looking sad. "And now with the Procedure only a couple of weeks away, it seems like a worse time again, but on the other hand . . . Oh, I don't know. Anyway, now I have to."

Mom turns to Bea and puts her shoulders back and says, "Beatrix, you had a twin. You had a twin brother who died a few days after you were both born." Bea is frozen. "His name was Benedix"—she does a little sob-laugh—"that was your father all over, that was, Beatrix and Benedix . . . He was always taking things a little too far, like really using names that started as a joke, or going ahead with an experiment when there was still so much unknown about . . ." She waves her hand, like, I can't go into that now. "Anyway, Ben, your brother, he had a problem with his lungs. They said he would only live a few hours, but he hung on for two whole days. Then he died." She stops talking for a second, and I can hear the clock on the bookshelf and the four of us breathing. "He was so small. You both were. Too small to die. Too new to be done." My throat squeezes. "I've been thinking about him since Saturday. Seeing you, Felix, inside that machine . . ." Her face begins to crumple up. "You are too new to be done too. And I'm scared. I'm not supposed to tell you that, I guess, according to the parenting rules, but I'm scared." She does a little shrug with her hands and then just sits there and cries.

We are not much of a touching family, but now my feet start shuffling me toward her, and Bea gets up and comes over too, and Mom puts her arms around both of us and clutches us to her and sobs. Bea is not crying but she's looking more and more uncomfortable, and my eyes are stinging. Grandy is standing behind Mom with a hand on her shoulder. Veir cheeks are wet. Bea breaks out of the huddle first. "You could have told me sooner," she says, and I can't tell if she is mad or sad or both. She turns and starts up the stairs. "Beatrix," Mom says, and Bea says, "Leave me alone," and she is gone. We hear her door close, click not slam.

Mom stands at the bottom of the stairs for a second but doesn't go up. Instead she goes into the bathroom and I hear the faucet running. When she comes out her face is pink with a few wet hairs plastered to her cheek. She goes into the kitchen and starts cleaning up, and then, as I mentioned, a whole day happens and here we are a day later.

I had a brother. Or I would have had, if he had lived until I was born. An older brother. It's so strange, I can't make it make sense.

13 Days to Go

Since the Big Family News, it has been business as usual—morning school home dinner—except for all of us in the Yz family being a little extra nice to each other. The other thing that has been going on is that I haven't been thinking about ZeroDay much because this threeness of things paper wouldn't let me alone, so during study hall I went to the library and finished my draft. It's pretty good, I think.

I explained the general idea of threenesses first, and I put in the stuff that Grandy said about the Trinity and the Dialectic (and, duh, obviously, I looked them up), and then I put in Hector (with his permission, which was nice of him, and we might have had another conversation too, but we only had a minute between classes), and I wrote about Grandy switching between Vera and Vern, and about the Story version of brain injury and the Procedure. I wanted to do Bea's secret twin, too, but I didn't think I could without asking, and with the news still so fresh I didn't feel like I could ask. Then I finished by trying to describe the vision I had when I was in the Apparatus. Actually, I mostly just used what I wrote here about it. I didn't have to do much except take out the snarky comment about school.

dance

You know, for a supersmart alien with a big word collection, you sure do use the same few over and over again.

swoop

Yeah, that's different.

whirligig

What? Where did you get that one?

helix

Hey, Felix helix. Cool.

curlicue arabesque whorl

Hoo boy, I'm sorry I said anything. Hush now?

. . .

Thanks. Anyway, I finished the paper in time to get it to Ms. C after school, and she said she would e-mail me comments as early in the evening as she could so that I could do a rewrite, and now I'm in my room waiting for the you've-got-mail chime. So far she hasn't gotten back to me.

Funny how intense I've gotten about this. Yeah, of course there's this big scary thing that I don't want to think about, so obviously my brain appreciates the distraction, but besides that, I think I might really like writing. It's so cool when my fingers get typing at the same speed as the thoughts forming in my head, and I like the game of finding the right word for each thought just fast enough to keep the flow going. It's also fun to use mostly normal everyday words, and then every once in a while just for the heck of it toss in a grandiloquent one. Like that. And, here's Bea.

Me: "Hey."

Bea: "Hey. What are you doing?"

"Typing every word we're saying. Zyx kinda helps me, so I can go really fast."

"Don't."

"Why not?"

"Because, because . . . oh, whatever. Do it if you want."

"OK, I will."

"So you do that."

"So OK, I will."

Silence. Now she's closing the door and sitting down with her back against it. More silence.

"What's up, Be-have?" (That's an old joke name, from Mom lecturing us when we were smaller.)

She's plucking fuzz out of the carpet. "Oh, you know . . . this twin thing."

"Yeah."

"I don't know how I'm supposed to feel, y'know?"

"Uh-huh."

"But it does explain a few things. Like when we were little, Mom was so overprotective sometimes. She would get freaky about the stupidest things—"

"Juggling chainsaws . . . eating fire in the living room . . ."

A little smile. "Running chainsaws, yeah. 'You take the gas out of that, young lady, this instant!'"

"'But not near the fire-eater torch lighting . . . thing! Far away from the fire!'"

We both laugh, but when she blinks, a tear runs down. She goes on: "It's almost too much. Because, there *you* are, about to get zapped, and all of a sudden there has already been this other death in the family. This other other death in the family, 'cause, Dad. I don't know if I can handle it."

It takes me a second to answer, because I don't want my voice to wobble. "Do you ever think about him?" Meaning, Dad.

She keeps her eyes down. "Sometimes, I guess. Mostly I have dreams." She pinches her sleeve to her hand and uses it to wipe her cheeks. "It's always something like, it turns out he's not dead after all, he's just been away for a long time and now he's back, but instead of it being happy, it's all dark and scary, because I don't know him anymore. He's changed. He's a stranger with this closed-off face, but we still have to pretend to be glad that he's back. Sucky, sucky dreams."

I nod. Long silence.

"Felix."

"Yeah?"

"What do you think he would have been like?"

"Ben."

"Yeah."

"Dunno. I guess it would depend. I can't remember, do twins always have to look alike?"

"I don't think so."

"But maybe he would look like you. So, you know, tall and skinny with dark hair—"

"Like you, you mean."

"Me, tall?"

"Looked in a mirror lately? And since we're talking about it, gonna start shaving sometime soon? You're starting to look kinda scraggly."

"Scraggly?"

"Scraggly."

"What if I like it that way?"

"Whatever."

"OK, sure, like me then. But older. He would be sixteen, like you."

"He was older than me, Mom said. By twelve minutes."

"So that makes you . . . dun-dun-daaahh! The middle child."

"I suppose. Whatever." More silence. "I wonder, would we have had one of those special mystical bonds that twins are supposed to have? A psychic connection?"

"Like a threeness? You and him and the bond between you?"

That's good for an eye-roll. "I suppose."

"I could still put that in my paper. Can I put that in my paper? Please please please?"

"OK, I guess."

"Thanks."

She ponders. "You know, I've always had this feeling that there was something . . . left out, something incomplete. An empty place."

"You've never said anything about it."

"Well, I have."

"Are you sure? Sure you're not making it up in, whadayacall, retrospect?"

She looks hurt. "I say I felt it, and I felt it. You don't have to be so—"

"OK, sorry."

Loooooong silence. At last she looks up. "Felix."

"Yeah?"

"You better survive this. I don't think I could stand to lose another brother." We look in each other's eyes. Feels . . . feels with wheels. I start to get squirmy and look away first, and right then the computer chimes, so I click, and it's Ms. C's e-mail, and the first little preview bit looks good: "Felix, overall this is a remarka—"

While I was glancing, Bea got up and opened the door, and now she's gone. What's left is the feel of that last look still in the air.

12 Days to Go

Aaaaand, it has been another evening of chess and social awkwardness. Huzzah.

most pretty chess yet

Yeah, you liked playing against Ursula, didn't you?

fun fun fun

Yeah. See if you can channel your glee until I catch up, will you?

. . .

Thank you. So, first of all, Ms. C's e-mail last night: except for some spelling and grammar issues, she said my paper was already good. She did have some ideas about moving parts around, and maybe she was right, so I moved the parts, and I added Bea's twin thing. Also I fiddled with the end, because I keep thinking about the me-shaped shell and not being able to tell going down inside from rising up out of, and I wanted to get it just right. And this morning when I handed it in, I found out the winners will be announced just two days before the Procedure. I hope I win, and I'm glad I'll know, but, Mother Hubbard, what if I can't attend the awards ceremony on account of being dead?

OK, that was supposed to be a joke, but I had to go into the bathroom for a bit.

not fun

No kidding. The waiting and not knowing part. Definitely not fun at all.

The other thing I have been working on is this question: Should I, you know, say something to Hector? About liking him? To which the answer is sdslaksdjflskjdlksfdjd or, in other words, not dealing with that right now. Not not thinking about it, but not dealing with it.

Anyway. Chess.

We had dinner early so that the visit would be after, and right after we cleared the table, the doorbell rang. Rick is not quite at the just-walk-in stage yet, and may never reach it now—but I'm getting ahead of the story again. Just tell. Yes.

So, we're gathered in the dining room, planning ahead for computers. The whole family is there. I'm already twitching and unable to talk because Zyx is riled, so Bea gets the door, and we hear her talking and Rick's voice answering, and then a new voice speaks, and you can tell by the rhythm of it that the speaker is from somewhere else besides the United States. Then Bea leads our visitors into the kitchen.

Chess seems to be mostly a man thing, so I guess I was expecting a more man-looking woman than Ursula Ots turns out to be. My first impression is of a lot of blond hair, not super-neatly brushed, tied back at the back of her neck. Then I think some kids at school might call her fat, but she doesn't look like she would care what those kids think. She's wearing jeans and a long-sleeve shirt that are both pretty tight, so you can see she is definitely woman-shaped. Her eyebrows are browner than her hair, and she has big dark eyes that look like she's laughing even when she is being polite and serious saying hello.

Some bustling happens with Bea fetching another chair and Mom offering coffee, which Ursula accepts, and Mom going to get it and Rick setting up the tablet and another laptop they brought. He sets up the two machines opposite each other on the table, so the people sitting at them are facing each other like over a real chessboard. I sit and twitch and wonder if I will be able to say anything. Rick introduces Ursula to me and we shake, and her hand is the same size as mine and warm and feels soft and strong at the same time. Then she sits in the chair next to me and smiles and says, "So, Felix, you play chess."

Gah. The Story, can't talk about Zyx, blah blah blah—but I've rehearsed. Also, Zyx has pulled back a bit—thanks, Zyx—

welcome understand why

. . . so I can talk pretty normally, and I say, "I guess, yeah. But it's, like, a separate part of my brain or something."

"I see. Do you understand what you are doing when you play?"

"No." It's such a relief to be able to say this, but at the same moment Zyx makes my whole body convulse. Ursula ignores the jolt. I like talking to her—she's another person with the brain-eye-eye-brain thing going on. "All right, that's fine," she says. "Suppose we play some games?"

I guess Rick is maybe a little afraid of Ursula, because he hasn't said anything, but he has finished setting up the computers, so now there's a chessboard on the tablet in front of me with my Felix1 name listed as one of the players. The other player's name is Keisrinna, which is apparently Ursula's chess-site name. She has a GM after her name, for Grandmaster. Rick says, sounding eager to please, "I did three-minute games because of the mouse," and I guess he means if we play one minute per player like before, Ursula will be at a disadvantage because she's moving with a mouse, which takes a little longer than tapping the tablet. Rick also mentions that he has turned off watching for our games, so there will be nobody making comments this time. Just us, all private.

Ursula goes around the table and sits down, and Zyx flings my hands up on the tablet and moves just like that, because we're white and have the first move. Ursula looks startled for a moment, then nods at me and says, "Good luck." Then she moves her mouse and clicks and I see a pawn jump out to meet our pawn, and off we go.

Ursula playing chess sits hunched forward, frowning, holding still except for little movements of her eyes and head. I notice another thing: Rick showed me before how each player has a rating, a number that says how good vo is, and Ursula's rating is higher than anyone Zyx has played before. And I guess she really is a stronger player, because for the first time Zyx actually takes a couple seconds to makes some moves *take time see pretty*

Uh-huh. After the first six or seven moves, Ursula starts thinking more and more, just like the other players, and the longest of Zyx's think times *not think see pretty*

Well, then, the amount of time Zyx needs to bliss out on the game *yes bliss yes*

Gah, let me finish?

. . .

As I was saying, the longest amount of time Zyx needs to bliss out on any one move is still only a few seconds, and pretty soon Ursula is almost out of time. The board is covered with pieces—I can see at least three that can take other pieces, but other than that it's a confusing mess—and Ursula says, "Resign." She clicks with her mouse, and the message pops up: "Black resigns. Felix1 wins." She looks at me and nods, not seeming even a little upset that she lost. "You are very quick" is all she says. And then, "Again, yes?" And we play again.

This time Ursula has the white pieces, and she makes a different first move, one of the pawns on the edge, forward just one square. She glances up as she does it, like, See what you think of this, hey?

Well, same rhythm as before. She moves we move, pause. She moves we move, pause. Ursula's face never changes. Same slightly frowny expression, same little darts of the head. This game ends quickly because she clicks the mouse and then says, "Ah," and Zyx instantly moves, and she looks up and says, "Yes, that was a blunder," and she resigns again. I'm surprised—Grandmasters make mistakes? But I can't really show it, because Zyx is working me so hard.

So then we play five or six more games, one right after another, and Zyx wins every single one of them. Everyone is quiet, watching, except Rick making noises after some of Zyx's moves. Ursula always ends up either resigning or losing on time. It gets exciting at the ends of the time-loss games, because she can move fast when she has to, and Zyx always does, so the pieces are just flicking all over the place.

Finally there is a game that gets down to a time rush, and this time Zyx checkmates Ursula, and at last she betrays a reaction. "My God," she says with a little laugh. "I didn't even see it. Beautiful mate!" Her king is out in the middle of the board and only a few of our pieces are near it, but after a minute I can see that each square it can move to is covered by exactly one of ours: a couple of pawns, a knight, the bishop that did the checkmate move, our king—and the last square her king could run away to has one of her own pawns on it, blocking the way. Nowhere to run, kingy-pie. Checkmate. Cool.

Ursula sits back and stares at me, rubbing her fingers over her lips. Rick says, "Didn't I tell you? Didn't I tell you?" Ursula nods. Then she says, "This is unschooled and unconventional chess— no knowledge of opening theory, naturally—but then there is no need, because, Felix, you are faster than any human I have ever seen, and more elegant and artistic than any computer. Also, your play appears to be entirely without error. This is truly remarkable chess. It is even miraculous chess." She looks at Mom. "Ms. Yz," she says, "I would have to play more games with him to feel sure of what he can do, but it is clear that Felix is a prodigy. One of the most gifted, it would not be too much to say, that the world has ever seen." She looks at me again with a hard expression. "And, Felix, you say you cannot speak to me of what you are doing? You cannot tell me anything?"

I sit there groping for something to say, and then all of a sudden my hands, which are still on the tablet, start typing—there's a chat window—and Zyx is answering. Vo types, "*chess pretty.*"

pretty pretty beautiful

Yes, you can't seem to get over that, can you? But you had no business talking to her like that.

question mark

Gah! Because of the Story, because if the truth gets out, who knows what kind of trouble we'll get into with the Powers?

no worries

That's easy for you to say.

not know think same

You mean, she didn't know it was you. She thought it was all me. But there I was, not able to talk and typing instead, and it must have seemed so bizarre . . . but, yeah, the whole thing was already so bizarre, a little more probably wasn't going to hurt. I hope.

Anyway, now Ursula and Zyx have a conversation. In response to Zyx typing "*chess pretty*," Ursula says (out loud, not typing back), "Yes, it is beautiful. A contest and an art form and sometimes even a medium of wit."

"*wit question mark*" types Zyx, and at this point Mom makes a sound like starting to protest, but Grandy puts a hand on her arm. Grandy says to Ursula, "It's a question." Then vo turns to me, but I've never felt more strongly that someone was talking to Zyx instead of me, and says, "One way to define 'wit' would be, 'joy in the play of the patterns of life.'"

"*yes yes yes all joy all play beauty pretty pretty*"

Ursula stares at me even harder. "So," she says, "for you it is not about winning?"

"*not win dance*"

"You like the play for its own sake, then. The combinations, tactics, strategy."

"*question mark question mark question mark*"

Grandy says, "Different words for the patterns the pieces make."

"Yes, just so," says Ursula.

"yes yes pretty patterns dance forever"

Ursula opens her mouth to speak again, but Mom gets in first. "This has gone far enough," she says. Ursula looks at her and Mom looks back, and then the look stretches out until all of a sudden Mom's hand jumps to her throat at the same moment that Ursula's eyebrows and lip corners twitch up, just for an instant. It happens so fast, I'm not even sure I saw it. Ursula starts doing computer-shutting-down moves with her mouse.

Rick is not ready to quit. "This is incredible," he says, and his voice is shaking. "Absolutely incredible. We're going to make a fortune. . . ." Then he tapers off, because the look on Mom's face says she's close to blowing her top. She doesn't get mad often, but when she does, it can definitely be a thing. There's this tense silence while Ursula closes her laptop and stands up. She clears her throat and smiles. "If I may say something?" she asks uber-politely.

After a second Mom does a tight little nod.

"I would only remark that I am slated to play in an exclusive online tournament next Thursday. Some of the very best players in the world will be in it. The participants have been determined, but I would be willing to communicate to the organizers that I would like to yield my place to Felix." Silence. She adds, "It is a rare opportunity, and because of what I have seen this evening, I think Felix could place well. Even win." She shakes her head, and for the first time I see a look like wonder on her face. "He is chess talent such as I have never seen before."

There is a silence that starts to stretch uncomfortably, but then Grandy steps in, doing the mild slightly smiling thing vo does so well. "We'll think about it," vo says, and then everyone is leaving. It looks for a second like Rick is angling to stay—they came in separate cars—but then he looks at Mom's face again and goes out with Ursula.

11 Days to Go

It's so odd: in eleven days I might be dead, but I was still excited to wake up this morning, on account of MainahCon. I've been looking forward to it for weeks, even before Hector told me about Ash and about maybe being there himself, so I woke up without Mom calling me. Then I lay there for a little while in this clean dim gray light that I usually don't wake up early enough to see. The countdown part of my brain just wanted to hide behind my chair and whimper, but another part of my brain was still like, Yay, MainahCon, and the yay part came out on top, so I decided to get up.

Of course, even as we pull up to the convention center I'm already scanning for Hector. It's tricky because I don't know if he cosplays and if he does as what character, so I can't just scan for his hair and color and Hector-shape, I have to look hard at everyone. I don't see him anywhere. Once we're inside I also immediately start scanning for Ash's table. I don't see it at first and I start to wonder if Hector got it wrong, but then I catch sight of the Novaglyph symbol on a banner, and there she is.

Ash turns out to be a person of medium height with black hair buzzed short on one side, a nose ring, and tats on her hands and neck. She's wearing layers of mostly black clothes and an unusual hat, and she has a loose floppy way of sitting in her chair, like she's actually a rag doll instead of a human. She doesn't have much on her table—a stack of comics and some stickers and stuff—and she's flopped there, watching the people walk past.

By this time Bea has gone off on her own, so it's just me and Grandy. My heart starts to beat faster and I step closer to Grandy, who is in Vern mode, it being Saturday, with boots and jeans and a big belt buckle. Vo knows my fandoms and says, "There she is. How about it, Felix? Shall we approach?"

"Um. I'm feeling shy."

"Yes, but you can still go talk to her."

"I wish I had brought my sketchbook. No, I'm glad I didn't."

"Come on," Grandy says, and vo puts a hand on my shoulder and steers me forward.

When we get to the table Ash looks up and says, "Hey." Her voice is gentle and soft and her face looks sad, but her eyes are calm. All I can do is nod. "What's your name?"

"Felix."

"Hey, Felix," she says, and smiles, and her smile is sweet and also sad.

We look at each other for a second and then her head drops a little and her eyes go away and I think, Hm, maybe she's shy too, and that makes it possible for me to say, "I love your—"

"Thanks," she says. "Wanna sticker or something?"

"Yeah, thanks."

"You draw, Felix?"

I look at her face again, and this time her eyes stay on mine and she does the sad smile again and this little shrug with one shoulder, like, Yo, we're just talking, so I start twitching and stuttering, trying to say something about Jarq, and she's nodding and listening, and then because I know it's safe I say, "If I had brought my sketchbook I could show you," and Grandy's hand comes over my shoulder holding veir phone with one of my drawings on the screen and I make a noise that is supposed to mean, No, stop! but it's too late and the phone is in Ash's hand and she's swiping, swiping, nodding, and I look up at Grandy with my eyes burning like laser beams, but vo looks right back, so I add a snarl-face, but vo points veir eyes at Ash, and when I look back at her she says, "These are good. I like how you use perspective. And your shading is excellent."

Wow. Wow. I feel like I have fireworks going off in my body, but I'm back to not being able to speak.

Then she turns her head sideways and scrunches up her eyebrows and asks in a hesitating way, "How do you feel about your proportions?"

What? She can see that? Of course she can, she's Ash Cortez. But I've already stepped the last step to the table. She turns the phone so we can look at the screen together, and all of a sudden I can talk. I tell her about how hard it is to get the shoulders and arms and hips and legs to work right, something's always too long or short or big or small or just shaped wrong somehow, and she tells me how she spends all this time drawing her characters doing odd things they won't ever do in the comic, standing on their heads, doing somersaults, scratching their butts, and my brain goes Kaboing! because it's such a good idea, and . . . well, anyway, we have this amazing conversation and the fireworks just keep going off and all of a sudden I feel like I'm about to cry, so I do this sudden awkward good-bye and we walk away and my face is burning but she gives me one last smile and says, "Nice to meet you, Felix. Keep on keepin' on," and, and, well, it was incredible, the whole thing.

Nelson, I just had to go into the bathroom again. Never mind not having enough time to draw everything I want to draw, I don't even have time to draw anything I want to draw. Gah. A thousand times gah. And I never saw Hector, but Grandy went back to Ash's table and got me a comic, and it's so cool to see the art on paper instead of only on a screen. I would say maybe I could see my art on paper someday too, except my life is probably already over. How can things be so amazing and so horrible at the same time? This living stuff, it hurts worse than dying. I'd rather be dead. No, that's not true. I . . . I . . . GAAAAAAAH!

Yeah, you know what? I'm done for today. The words just don't work anymore right now.

10 Days to Go

So you might have noticed I got a little stressy again yesterday at the end of my entry. That's because I wasn't completely truthful when I wrote about getting up yesterday morning. I just said I decided to get up, which makes it sound easy, but it wasn't easy. I left out so much, it was really the same as a lie.

lie question mark

Are you kidding? Remember I tried to explain to you before? It's as bad as jokes. You are never going to get it.

. . .

Good. Anyway, I did wake up on my own in the gray light, like I said, and I was able to pry my eyes open, barely, but other than that I couldn't move at all. I was locked up worse than ever before—even breathing hurt—and this time when Mom finally came upstairs I couldn't break out of it and she found me like that. In a couple of minutes the whole family was clustered around the chair trying to help me move, and finally, with their help, I was able to do it, but it felt like actually breaking things. Then I had to admit that the lockups have been happening for a while and Mom got mad and made a phone call and now Dr. Yoon and everyone at the Facility know too, and they're saying given this new information, it's a lot more likely than they thought before that if we don't do this, Zyx and I will both die, but they can't move the date up because they're already getting the Apparatus ready as fast as they can. And then there was the part of the phone call where Mom's face went slack and she said, "As bad as that," and when I asked her after what she meant, her eyes got skittish and she said that Dr. Yoon had said that the chances of dying from the Procedure were also higher than they thought before, and I said how much higher, and she said one in five, and I said a one in five chance that I'll die and she kept her face down and nodded.

So I've been all la-de-da, there's a slight chance this might go badly but it's worth the risk, when actually I'm probably screwed either way. Great. Fabulous. Wonderful. And, Zyx, don't you type a word. I don't want to hear from you right now. I don't want to think about it, and I don't want to type about it anymore myself.

•••

It's later and I've been kicking around, being crabby and stuff, and I'm realizing that even though I don't want to write about looming death, I still want to write about something. I've gotten into the habit. So, how about some more backstory instead? I've been thinking about the time right after the accident, and Grandy is here and says vo'd be happy to narrate for Zyx the magic typist, so here we go:

"It was a complicated and frightening time. Your mother was practically mad with grief over your father, and for several days the doctors thought you were going to die. Recall that we had not the least inkling at first about the presence of our new friend *zyxilef in our lives . . ."

[Um, better explain that: *zyxilef is Zyx's full name. The * is a new letter Grandy invented. It stands for a cork-pop sound you make with your lips. The rest is my name spelled backward—also a Grandy invention (of course). Vo says since my name ends with XYZ, and since that's like the X and Y and Z axes in a graph of three-dimensional space, we needed another letter for Zyx's extra dimension. But it's hard to make a Z sound right after a cork-pop sound, so everyone but Grandy just says Zyx.]

". . . just an eradicated impetuous scientist and that scientist's young child so paralyzed as to be rendered practically incapable of breathing, let alone moving. They tried everything to revive you—drugs, mostly. That was hard to watch. You were still little older than a baby, and I couldn't bear to watch when they put the IV needle in your soft little arm.

"I was not there the whole time. Your mother was in another room the first day, sedated, and after that needed a good deal of looking after for several days. And, of course, I had my own grief to cope with too. Still, I ended up spending many hours at your bedside." Vo falls silent, then goes on more softly. "You were a heartbreaking sight, Felix. Your little body frozen in that bizarre posture. You looked like a statue of a child cast in bronze. As though you would ring if struck.

"Well, there we sat with the beeping of the heart monitor, and that truly horrible fluorescent light that leached the color out of your face so that you looked dead. I remember on the second day, I dredged up a little table lamp from somewhere, to add some yellow to all that gelid blue. I had no idea if you could hear or understand me, but in case you could, I talked to you. I made up silly stories about a two-dimensional frog—"

"Tidy Teddy, 2-D Toad. I typed out one of the stories the other day. Zyx helped me."

"Why, yes, that's right. I'm so pleased you remember." Vo pauses a moment, I guess to enjoy feeling pleased. "In any case, for many days nothing we did seemed to have any effect whatsoever. Then, finally, one morning Dr. Yoon was there, shining her penlight into your eyes and such, the way she did, when we both heard a little sound, just the least little squeak. We both leapt to your bedside and looked into your face, and we saw a flicker of movement in your eyes. I neglected to mention before, you did occasionally blink, but this was different. This seemed to be a sign of returning life. Then you started working your jaw muscles, and then, finally, you whispered one word of two syllables, with such a long pause between them that it took us a minute to figure out what you were saying. And you know what you whispered. . . ."

I've heard the story before, of course. "Firs . . . tee."

"Yes, that's right. My dear grandchild wanted a drink of

water." Grandy swipes a finger at the edge of veir eye. "I still get emotional when I think of it, because that was the moment we began to hope that we weren't going to have to lose you, too.

"Dr. Yoon didn't want you trying to swallow liquid water, but when she held an ice chip to your lips, your jaws prized open enough to admit it, and your eyes flickered again as it melted in your mouth, and your throat worked, and we were on our way.

"The news of your returning speech and movement revived your mother more than anything else could have done, and from then on she was constantly at your bedside. We all were. We talked with you, played with you, and especially we read to you—long hours of reading. Sometimes I held you in my lap, and I still remember the curious stiffness of your body against mine.

"What we thought we were doing was teaching you to move and speak again, but what we were mostly doing, without realizing it, was teaching *zyxilef to move and speak. Veir presence in our lives finally came to light about three months after the accident. Dr. Gordon had come to see you, and he had brought with him a laptop, which was a much rarer object in those days—still something to exclaim about. He sat beside your bed and began typing, and your hands shot out and grabbed the computer with tremendous strength. Dr. Gordon tried to grab it back, but your mother said, 'No, wait,' and your hands found the keyboard and twitched and stuttered there. At first you produced only gibberish on the screen, but then letters started appearing more than other symbols, and then words. The first words were 'go goo good,' which is marvelous— a found poem—and then your body went very still and your fingers painstakingly typed, 'goodnight nobody,' which is a line from the book Goodnight Moon. Your mother had just been reading it to you.

"Uproar, consternation—The child has learned to parrot back words seen on the page, we all exclaimed—and then you, except, of course, it was dear *zyxilef, typed the words 'here now all,' and a look went between Drs. Gordon and Yoon, because apparently they had some idea by then of what might be happening, and Dr. Yoon said, 'Is that someone besides Felix typing?' and *zyxilef typed 'not felix,' and that was the beginning of figuring out what had truly happened to you and to *zyxilef and to us all.

"Dear *zyxilef. It has been such a curious pleasure and honor to have you in our lives."

What? Oh, Grandy is talking straight to Zyx now. Guess that makes me the telephone. Joy.

zyx love grandy

That gets a smile. "Grandy love Zyx." Silence. Grandy clears veir throat. "*zyxilef, there's a question I have long wanted to ask you. May I ask it?"

yes

"To your knowledge, has there ever been any other connection between our two planes? Any communication, any comings and goings?"

yes

"Oh, good. I thought so. Or I hoped. Can you tell us anything about it?"

not know how say

"Ah, yes, these foolish words of ours. You must find them so cumbersome. Very well, leaving aside the specifics, if connection has happened before, could it happen again?"

yes

"In any way we can control, make happen?"

maybe

"How?"

round round round

"I beg your pardon?"

round round round sing sing sing

Grandy and I stare at each other and all of a sudden veir eyes widen, and I wonder if it's a look of fear I see on my Grandy's face. It's hard to be sure, because it's a look I've never seen before. Vo drops veir eyes and says, just a little flustered-sounding, "Well, perhaps some things are better left unknown," and that's the end of the conversation.

Still 10 Days to Go

It's Sunday night, and I just got offline with Hector. It should've been amazing—our first chat, and he began it—but it wasn't. It was the opposite of amazing. How can I explain what happened? I guess I will just cut and paste the whole chat. Gah. Gah times infinity.

Before I do that, though, the other thing that has been going on is the family talking about whether I should play in Ursula's chess tournament. Mom is still saying no because she's mad at Rick, but Grandy is reminding her of her own idea of me getting to see and do things I wouldn't otherwise get to see and do. I'm staying out of it, because right now I can't make myself care. Of course Zyx wants to play, and if you're going to say chess pretty, you can save it *chess pretty*

Or not.

Anyway, besides the Hector chat disaster and the great chess debate, the other other thing that has been going on today is the heavy-arms-heavy-legs feeling has come back again. The joy just seems to have drained out of everything.

Can I be honest? Express my feelings the way the therapists say we're supposed to do?

yes

Rhetorical . . . never mind.

All right, here it is.

I'm afraid.

Again.

Still.

The Procedure is only ten days away.

I may only have ten days left to live.

Shouldn't something, you know, more important be happening? Instead of just another boring day do your homework keep up appearances continue to act normal WHATEVER THAT MEANS! I DON'T KNOW WHAT IT MEANS AND I DON'T CARE AND ANYWAY I DON'T WANT TO BE NORMAL WHATEVER IT MEANS! I WANT TO BE ME! AND I DON'T WANT TO DIE!

OK, I'm back. I've never cried like that in my life before. I cried so hard, I choked. No one could hear me—the door was closed—so I lay curled up on the floor and about puked my guts out. G. A. H. I need a drink of water, and to wash my face.

zyx love felix

You shut up. That's not going to work this time. I'm taking my hands away now so you can't type.

Back, but I'm still not letting you type, Zyx, and I don't feel like being honest and expressing my feelings anymore tonight. So here's my chat with Hector. I can't believe I hit enter on the one line, but it's just so automatic. And make sure to pay attention to when it's H and when it's F with mixed-case typing and when it's F with all lowercase typing (no italics this time—you'll have to figure it out for yourself). It's important if you want to understand how badly everything sucks.

H: Hi

F: Oh, hi. You surprised me with your window popping up there.

H: This ok?

F: Yeah sure. Didn't see you at the con.

H: I was there

F: When?

H: Last couple hours. We were late

F: Oh. That's why. We left early. I looked for you.

H: Cool

H: So how u doin?

F: OK. Bad mood.

H: :(

F: Tx. Just kinda black . . .

H: No wonder

F: You mean, with the procedure coming?

H: Yah

F: You mean yeah?

H: I mean yah. What, you the spelling police now?

F: No. It just looks like something else. Like, yah, you moron.

H: No, just how I spell yah

F: OK then.

H: Ok

F: So how are you? What are you doing?

H: Ok homework hanging out

F: Me too. Except for the homework part. I just can't seem to care right now, you know?

H: I'm serious about school. I want to get into nursing school, and competition is tough

F: You want to be a nurse?

H: Yah. I want to go do nursing in Haiti

F: Cool.

H: What do you want to be?

F: I don't know. At this point I'd settle for alive.

H: :(

H: You there?

F: Yeah.

H: You didn't answer for a while

F: Yeah sorry, I was thinking about something.

H: What

F: felix love he No shut up stupid

F: Hector, are you there?

F: Hector

H: Don't you ever call me stupid. Ever

F: I'm so sorry, I wasn't talking to you.

H: Who were you talking to?

F: It's hard to explain. Gah, this is going to sound so dumb . . . it's like there's this other me inside me because of the you know

H: Yah right Felix well you know what take responsibility for yourself. Forget it I'm gone

F: Hector

F: Hector?

F: Hector?

Zyx, I'm going to kill you.

no kill why kill

I was talking to him. You had no right to butt in.

butt in question mark

I barely stopped you from making it look like I said I love him.
One more letter and it would have been for sure.

felix love hector

That's not the point! You can't just blurt it out like that.

why not blurt

Because I don't know if he . . . I mean, just to say it like that
in the middle of some random chat . . . I mean, what can he
be thinking of me right now? And what am I going to say the
next time I see him? That's not going to be awkward, nooooo,
not even a little bit.

question mark

I cannot even begin to explain. Talking about love might be all easy and perfect in your dimension, but not in mine. And I'm done. See you later good night bye. Sleep, wake, a day closer to death, tra-la.

9 Days to Go

I get so afraid I'm going to die. Then I start to hope. Then the fear comes back—whammo—and I feel like I want to destroy everything or just explode. And look: the words come out the same. They're just regular words. Do they even work? Can they possibly say how incredibly awful my life is right now?

I'm going to die.

I'M GOING TO DIE!

im going to die

(That's me this time being all e e cummings, not Zyx.)

Hey kids, guess what? I'm going to die! Isn't that exciting? Yay!

OMG, this is so awesome!!!!! I'm going to die!!!!! :-D :-D :-D :-D :-D

Words are so strange.

Morning was a happy happy time. Mom was crabby because, I admit, it took me a while to get out of my chair. Not completely locked up again, so that at least was not as bad as it could have been, but just not interested in getting up. Or eating, or going to school, or anything really. And Bea was all disappeared inside herself, I guess still thinking about Ben, which I would be too if my head wasn't full of looming death.

So then tense silence in the car, Mom driving us because we're late, and then I'm hurrying inside the building and Tim the Bore shows up out of nowhere and smashes my books out of my hands and then totally gets in my face: "Felix the retard, Felix the moron, Felix the i-di-ot-tuh!" And suddenly this hot red feeling rises up inside me, I guess it's rage, but it scares me and somehow I push it back down. I don't say a word. I gather up my books as fast as I can with him kicking them and stepping on the papers—the math worksheet I'm supposed to turn in has a big muddy sneaker print all over the front—and he's still going at it: "You better watch it, retard. You just wait. I'm going to put such a hurt on you.

You're going down. Come on—fight back. What's the matter with you? Fight back!"

I feel like my teeth are going to shatter, I'm biting down so hard, but I don't make a sound. My silence seems finally to confuse him or something, because he takes a step back, breathing hard, and glares at me, and I stare back, and I notice that he has a bruise over his eye, and for one second I feel the brain-eye-eye-brain thing happening, and I could swear that in that second I can see that he has some pain in him that is as big as the pain I have in me—which is a monster, a might-be-dying-in-nine-days monster—and he kinda flinches and looks away, and I walk past him, just brushing his shoulder, and go in to class. It takes me until the end of first period to stop shaking.

Then I get *spoken to* by two different teachers, once for staring out the window and once for drawing a big black cloud on a worksheet I'm supposed to be working on. The school feels too warm and I can smell myself and I smell rank, which makes me squirm. The rage is still humming just under the surface, ready to burst out again, and don't forget the heavy feeling, that black thing—it's still lurking all the time too—so the color scheme of the day is red and black. And on top of all that, I also feel practically ripped in half by the equal and opposite pulls of wanting to see Hector really badly and talk to him, and having no idea what I would say and feeling like if he even looks at me I will die.

So maybe it's a good thing that the one time I see him during the day, way down at the other end of the long hall, even over all that distance he makes it clear that he's not going to give me the present of eye contact today. Same thing after school, too, at the buses. I see him walking and take a step toward him from the side, and he gives me one quick glance and then locks his eyes forward and puts his chin up so you can really see the line of his whole profile clearly against the school bus yellow (and can I really be noticing what I liked about him even in that moment? Yes, it appears that I can) and walks past without turning. I try to say his name, but nothing comes out but air, and feeling pulled in opposite directions and all that, probably it's just as well. But I still really want to talk to him.

what say

Oh, you're awake, are you?

never sleep

I know. Sarcasm.

. . .

I would say sorry. I would say, please let me explain. I would say, I have this stupid alien in my head. Not metaphorically. Really. And sometimes this stupid alien uses my hands to talk. And I can't say any of that, but I want to so badly.

[Five minutes of staring at the screen]

OK, so I hate the world and the world hates me. Fine. I don't want to think about it and I don't want to write about it. So I'm not going to.

Aaaaand, here's Mom.

Me: "Fair warning, I'm typing everything you say."

"You are? Why?"

"It's this honest writing thing I'm doing, and capturing detail."

"Oh. OK, I guess."

Awkward pause. Then, "Well, I just came to say, it's been getting warmer, so I changed the sheets on your chair today. I took the winter flannel ones off, and put the cotton ones on. And I changed out the heavy quilt for a lighter spring one."

I look at my recliner, and sure enough, the old quilt is gone. I didn't even notice. All of a sudden I have an ache in my throat so bad I can't speak.

She says, "Thank you?"

"Yeah, Mom, thanks."

"OK, sweetie."

She comes into the room and kisses my forehead, gives me a sad little smile, and goes away.

My mom is a good mom. She gets seriously stressy sometimes, but she's a good mom.

8 Days to Go

Home from school, and after yesterday I didn't think things could get any worse, but it turns out they could. Hector. I tried to talk to him, I really tried, and it went . . . well, see for yourself.

Scene: hallway, right after last bell. Lockers slamming, people talking and laughing, heading home. Hector has been avoiding me all day. Knowing where his locker is, I find him there. I approach. He gives me one look and then keeps his eyes away.

Me: "Hector." No answer. "Hector. Won't you at least talk to me?" Still no answer. "About what I said . . ."

Him, still not looking, his voice full of contempt: "Are you going to say it's not your fault? That there's some kind of alien inside your head?"

Me, drowning in absurd irony: "No. I'm sorry I called you stupid."

At last he looks at me, but his face is cold. "You're sorry."

"Yeah."

"Well, fine then. Whatever." He turns away. "Doesn't really matter."

"Do you mean like, no big deal, or because you don't . . ." Hector slams his locker and starts walking away, so now I have to tag after him.

"I mean, it doesn't really matter."

Now I'm starting to feel mad. "OK, fine. No big deal."

"That's right. You're just some kid I know a little. So yeah, no big deal." His eyes meet mine for one second, and what is it I see? Hurt, sad, angry? Maybe a mix of all, maybe none. I can't tell.

Now I let the mad take over. "Well, you don't have to be so touchy about it. See you around sometime maybe . . . or not," I say in a mean voice. Our eyes glance off each other again, and suddenly I want to grab him in my arms and I'm thinking, What the hell?

His mouth twists and he says just as mean, "I'm thinking not," and then he turns and walks away fast without looking back, and I stand there with my mouth flopping like a fish in air, thinking, What the hell??

felix love hector

You said that, remember? But yeah, I have to admit it. You're right. I'm in love with this boy, and he doesn't want to have anything to do with me, and I'm probably going to be dead in eight days.

My life sucks so bad.

There's the dinner call. Go down? Am I hungry? I can't tell. Oh well, I guess. It's something to do.

• •

After dinner, I mean after everyone else's dinner, I see a look go between Mom and Bea and then Bea leaves, not to play the piano but up to her room, and I think, Uh-oh, and then Mom and Grandy are both looking at me with *parental eyes*, and I know I am in for a Talk. Great.

I point my eyes at my plate, which still has all my food on it, and I notice that moving has started to feel hard again. Not lockup—the heavy black feeling again. It's hard now, too, typing this. I'm getting so tired. Even fingers heavy. Zyx, help me type.

Mom starts. "Felix, Grandy and I want to talk with you." I don't answer and the silence gets long. "And, for heaven's sake, what am I doing over here on this side of the table? You're not in trouble." She comes around to my side and pulls a chair close. She hovers a hand by my shoulder, like she's not sure whether I'll allow her to touch me, which is smart, because I'm not sure if I will. She decides to do it. I let the hand stay. "Felix," she says, all gentle, "I know how hard this must be for you. . . ."

I shrug her hand off. She hovers it again, then puts it in her lap with the other one. "All right," she says, "maybe I don't."

"No, you don't."

"Fair enough."

Grandy (in Vera mode, it being Tuesday) says, "But that doesn't mean we can't help you, dearheart."

Another silence gets long. Finally Mom again. "Sweetie, maybe it would help if you said something, if you expressed what you are feeling."

I don't answer, but inside I think, How do you put black infinity into words? Because I feel like that's what I'm on the edge of now.

You can't see how hard this typing is for me.

She waits and finally just to get her to stop looking at me like that I say, "You mean like that time with Penelope?" Who was a counselor she sent me to before. Let's just say it didn't go well. Pointless. Waste. Of. Time.

Lead weights.

Grandy says, "Not necessarily. Could be right now. Wouldn't have to be words, you know. A primal scream or throwing your plate at the wall might be good alternatives." That makes Mom twitch, but she doesn't say anything.

I look up at Grandy, and there's that cat smile of veirs. I hate that smile sometimes. I look back down again.

Black funnel going down.

Mom says, "That's right. It can help to express. Instead of keeping it all bottled up inside."

Same old happy talk. The black goes red for a couple seconds and I say, "Oh right. Like you kept Bea's secret twin bottled up inside." Mom jerks back. Grandy makes a little noise. I point my voice at ven. "And like I don't know your name." Somewhere inside I know that they are trying to help me and that I'm being mean, but this thing is rolling now. Can't stop. Mom puts her hand on my shoulder again, which is maybe the only thing that could get me moving. Suddenly I don't want anyone to touch me to talk to me to be near me. I want to go to my room and get in my chair and pull the covers over my head and maybe just die. Can you let go and die? If you really want to? Just let your heart stop beating?

not die

You shut up. Nobody asked you. So now here I am in my chair

and there is one little part of me left (not Zyx, I have other parts that are not Zyx) saying get up, if you keep lying here you really might die, you don't want that do you, but all the rest of me says whatever I don't care I just want to let go and sink down and now the only thing that's keeping me going is that I'm typing this and then I'll stop and then maybe I'll die no wait, here's Bea.

Bea: "Hey."

Me:

Bea: "Mom says you seem depressed."

Me:

A straw hits me. She threw a straw at me. Like we're in elementary school again, trying to cheer each other up. It makes me look at her, and her face is sad and frightened and full of love i guess, but i can't feel anything here comes the black going down into the funnel now too hard to type anymore too hard time to die i guess goodbye . . . .

6 Days to Go

Yesterday was the worst I have ever felt in my life.

dark

I guess you didn't like it either.

dark light two sides dance between

You know, sometimes . . . ah, never mind.

So, obviously I'm a little better now, because I can make my fingers move. I was in my chair all day yesterday. Not locked up—just didn't get up. Mom coaxed and then threatened, but I didn't answer, so she stopped talking and just sat for a while with a hand on my arm, which if I had been able to feel anything might have made me feel better, but I couldn't feel anything, only black.

I guess there was a phone call to Dr. Yoon because at some point Mom came with a pill and propped me up and washed it down my throat with some water. I dribbled on the pillow, so she changed it. Then I slept and dreamed that Mom and Grandy were standing in the doorway talking about me as though I was already dead, and I woke up in the dark, alone, and had a confused idea of dark inside and dark outside and the shell of me in the middle. It was like the idea I had in the Apparatus the other time, but that was all sparkly infinity, while this was cold dead emptiness. Here's the weird thing: it was comforting. At least in the way of not having to try anymore. I just wondered a little bit, like, Hm, that's odd, I'm not dead. How can I not be dead? Huh.

And then a little while ago there was another pill and now there's this weird glow on the edges of things and I feel like I can move again but other than that I don't feel good. But look, I'm typing this, so that must mean something I guess.

And here's the other thing: that chess tournament is tonight, and we already know what Zyx thinks about that so please don't say anything thank you for not saying anything, but I've gotten interested too. Oh hey, look, interested in something. So I must not be completely depressed anymore.

I'm heavy and floaty at the same time. Mother Hubbard, I feel strange. OK, I want hot water now. Shower.

•••

Aaaaand, it's late, but I have to stay up and describe what happened since this morning. Which was nothing most of the day. I didn't want to go to school and Mom didn't try to make me, so I spent most of the day lost in mindless websurfing. Just now though was the big chess tournament, Zyx playing against some of the best players in the world, and if there was time for the people who are all excited to do anything, there would be what Mom calls a brouhaha. Seeing as how in a week I'll either be dead or a really bad chess player again, though, that can't happen.

It was Rick and Ursula again, just like before, and the setup was the same with the two computers facing each other across the dining room table, but this time Zyx was playing against other people. Ursula was signed on to the other computer so she could observe. Rick sat with her. He was going to sit behind me, but I gave him a look that Mom read right, and she said something about giving me some space and he looked at her face and switched sides. Bea (with a book) and Grandy (in Vern mode, with knitting) were also there, watching.

While we're waiting for the start, Ursula explains that this is an elite bullet tournament the chess-playing site is putting on as a fund-raiser, so a whole bunch of people are going to be watching. I guess there are enough serious chess geeks on the Internet to make that work.

Bea says, "So if it's only an exhibition tournament, does that mean that the players won't really be trying?"

Ursula opens her mouth to speak, but Rick pushes in ahead of her. "Oh, don't worry about that," he says. "These guys always go for blood. It's what makes them the champions they are." Then he gives me a look like he's just imparted some great knowledge or something. Ursula makes a little pain-face, just for a moment, and says, "I would say rather that, as top-level players, they are incapable of playing at less than their best."

Tournament time comes, and the first game board pops up on the screen. The other player's name has a dash and GM after it. Everyone else playing in this tournament is a Grandmaster. Doesn't matter. Zyx rips ven to shreds, just like everyone else vo has ever played. Ursula and Rick do commentary, and I try to learn from what they're saying. Like one time Rick says, "That can't possibly be sound, saccing the knight like that." Bea says, "Sacking a knight? What do you do to a bishop? Bag it?" This makes me snort. Ursula says, "No, you misunderstand. Sac is short for sacrifice. And it was a sound sacrifice. In fact, a brilliant one."

The other thing going on is that there's a chat window next to the chessboard, and judging from how fast the comments are piling up, there must be a lot of people watching. Ursula clicks with her mouse and says more than two hundred people are observing our first game. Then Rick says talk is spreading in the Internet chess world about this new prodigy Felix1. So, people have come to check me, I mean Zyx, out.

Game one ends when the other person runs out of time, and there's a pause while other first-round games are finishing. In the chat window, people are guessing who I am. Rick and Ursula keep saying names and laughing, so I guess they are names of famous players. As I have mentioned, Ursula usually looks serious when she's at the chessboard, but when she laughs her whole face opens up and her eyes and teeth flash, and it occurs to me that she might be really funny. I notice Bea noticing too, and she wrinkles her nose at me—the good kind of nose-wrinkle.

Then a new screen pops up and we're off again, and I think this new player must be really good because from time to time Zyx actually seems to think for a second *not think see pretty*

Fine, same as before, Zyx pauses to bliss out on the complexity of the patterns *yes yes so deep*

. . . but still game two ends quickly, because the other person makes a mistake. "No, no," Ursula says, at the same time that Rick shouts, "What a blunder!" Ursula smiles at me, and this time it's Mom I notice noticing her smile, then Bea noticing Mom noticing Ursula's smile, and I'm the one who does the nose-wrinkle at Bea. Ursula says, "Felix, your reputation precedes you. Now you are winning games simply because you intimidate your opponents. They are rattled."

Then there is a longer wait because our game ended so quickly. Mom sets a plate of cheese and crackers and apple slices on the table and comes around with glasses of water, and when she gives Ursula her water Ursula touches her hand and thanks her, and Mom actually blushes. Noticing tree this time: me and Bea together noticing Mom blushing, then both of us noticing Rick noticing too, then me and Bea still together noticing that neither Mom nor Ursula has noticed Rick noticing. And this time the silent comment between us is, Uh-oh, complications maybe ahead. Of the romantic sort, for Mom.

Now there are more than five hundred people watching our games, and the comment stream has brought back the idea that maybe Zyx is a computer. Which, for all I know, vo may be.

not computer

OK, so not a computer, and not a god, either. Fine. What *are* you?

can not explain can show

You can show me what you are?

yes but maybe kill

Um, in that case, thanks but no thanks. ANYWAY, when the computer talk starts, Ursula types for a second, and I see her Keisrinna site name appear in the chat stream, and her comment is: "Felix is a human being. I am watching him play, and I can certify he is not using any computer assistance." And I guess she must be pretty big in the world of chess because there are some oh wow fangirly comments, and then the chat goes back to guessing names.

There are seven rounds in the tournament, and at the end of the sixth round there is only one player besides Zyx who has won every game. His name is Miguel something, but Rick says everyone calls him El Rey. He's like the rock star of the chess world, apparently—one of the very best players on the planet. He's from Argentina and he's only seventeen years old, and he's cocky as hell (those are Rick's words) and has a huge fan following. His specialty is this one-minute chess we are playing. Rick says he comes on the site at random times and plays everyone who dares to challenge him and wins game after game, and at the same time he's making jokes in the window, chatting with his fans. I guess he's also watching soccer on TV while he plays, because sometimes he comments on that, too.

So game seven is between Zyx and El Rey. There's a little pause, like the cyber-referees are making sure everything is ready, and then a board pops up and off we go. The big difference between this game and the others is, El Rey is almost as fast as Zyx. Not quite, but almost. The pieces on both sides are just going zip zip zippity zip, and all I can do is stare. In the first couple of seconds Ursula clicks and says quietly, "More than one thousand spectators," and then Rick screams, "He's lost, he's lost! You've got him! It's over!"

I guess El Rey doesn't like to lose because he keeps playing, but a bunch of white pieces are disappearing and then there's a final flurry of moves with his king dancing over to the side of the board all by itself, and then the dialog pops up, "White checkmated. Felix1 wins," and El Rey posts some really bad words in the chat stream and disconnects, and the tournament is over. Ursula, staring at the screen, whispers something in what I guess must be Estonian, and Rick is jumping all around the room and shouting, and Zyx lets go of me all at once and I realize that my whole body is shaking and covered with sweat, and I fall out of my chair onto the floor.

Well, there's a fuss then, with Mom and Bea helping me up, and Rick failing to calm down at all, and on the computer screen the chat window scrolling so fast with new comments that you can't read them, but you can see that there's a lot of all caps and exclamation points, and the two clocks on the chessboard show :19 left for El Rey and :46 for Zyx, which means the whole game only took fifty-five seconds.

The rest is a lot like the last time and pretty boring. Once I am on my feet again, Mom gets all steely and says the evening is over, and Rick has to be pushed out of the room by Ursula and Grandy, and then Mom turns the steely thing on me and tells me to go to my room and rest, which is fine because I am

happy to go, and now that I have typed this I'm going to sleep, as soon as I check the latest Novaglyph installment. I can't believe it's Thursday and this is the first I've thought of it. I forgot for three whole days. That has never happened before.

chess pretty

Yeah, chess pretty.

zyx love felix

Good night to you too.

5 Days to Go

If I ever go home again.

A lot has happened in a little while, and now I don't know what the hell I'm doing, so I better just start at the beginning and go right through to the end, because that's the only chance I have of making sense right now.

After last night's post Mom came upstairs and made me take another of Dr. Yoon's pills and I had wild loopy dreams with rainbow lens flares off of everything, which I didn't like at all. It wasn't like sleeping so much as getting beaten unconscious. On the other hand when I woke up I didn't feel lost in infinite blackness anymore, and I wasn't completely locked up either—I mean, it hurt, it always hurts, but I could move—so I counted that as a good morning and said no thanks when Mom offered me another pill. They're so little, those pills. Tiny white circles. Must be some powerful molecule.

So instead of black, I was back to red this morning. Red, as in rage. It started rising up inside me on the bus to school. I was staring out the window, watching the same houses and trees and telephone poles and the mini-mall and the gas station go by as always, and thinking, This could be the last time I'll ever see these things, because even if the plan wasn't to leave for the Facility on Monday, which it is, it's vacation next week. And that is just so insult added to injury. Not only do I have to go and maybe die, I'm not even going to get off from school to do it.

Saying I got mad doesn't say what it felt like. What it felt like was being stuck in the Titanic after it split in half and sank to the bottom of the Atlantic, and I'm trapped in a cabin, and it's pitch-dark and there's no way out, and the water is bubbling in, rising higher and higher, and the water is rage.

So we get to school and I zombie-walk inside and zombie-sit through math and English. If Hector is anywhere around I don't see him, but I'm not looking.

Then I'm walking to my locker after second period, and there's

Tim the Bore coming down the hall with his friend Chester. They angle toward me so that I'm going to have to squeeze by the lockers to get around them, and Tim lifts his hand up to smack my books out of my hand, and a sparkly red haze comes in around the edges of my vision, and when he starts to bring his hand down I drop the books ahead of the smack and grab his arm and lean back and swing him headfirst into the lockers. Makes a huge bang. He pinwheels back and I get a leg behind his stumbling feet and he's down on the floor. Chester comes at me and I push him so hard he falls down— the red haze has gotten thicker and begun to pulse—and then I get down on top of Tim and just start pounding on him. Then people are yelling and hands are pulling me off, and I get hauled into Dr. A's office.

Then there is a bunch of talk—teacher talk, grown-up talk. I don't pay attention. The red is draining down again, back down to black. My knuckles hurt from hitting Tim, and someone says he has been taken to the nurse's office.

After a while Mom turns up, looking sad and tired, with her hair in even more of a cloud than usual. She doesn't get mad, just looks at me with those tired eyes and shakes her head. She says something about the strain of our life just now, mentions the Procedure, and then there's no anger anymore, only grinched sad mouths and grown-ups nodding the way they do.

Then Mom takes me out to the car, where, surprise, Rick is sitting in the passenger seat. Oh, hello, Rick, what are you doing here? Whatever. Nobody talks on the way home. When we get there Mom tells me to go to my room in a way that isn't exactly an order, more like a stern suggestion, but I want to anyway. I get into my chair in all my clothes and sleep.

When I wake up I know some time has gone by because the light is different. What wakes me is the sound of voices—Mom and Rick not quite yelling, but talking loudly enough that I can hear it coming up through the floor. I ease my way to the top of the stairs so I can listen.

Rick says, "I don't think you understand how much of a miracle this is. Your son is probably the greatest chess genius the world has ever seen. He is going to *need* a manager, and I am perfect for the job."

Mom says, "I don't think . . . No, I know, you're the one who doesn't understand. Felix's procedure is next week, and . . . and I haven't been able to admit to him that I switched the numbers, that the one in five is his chance of surviving—"

"I understand, it's terrible, but, Margie, you can't stop planning for the future. Look, all I'm asking for is your agreement that if he survives, you'll let me be his manager. I know that world. I can—"

"You know what? That's enough. I can't believe you're talking about this right now."

One in five chance of surviving. It's like the last piece of a puzzle I didn't realize I was putting together, and all of a sudden I know: I'm leaving. If they can't find me, they can't kill me. Time to disappear.

I pull out my camp duffel and throw some clothes into it. I tiptoe out to the bathroom and grab my toothbrush and toothpaste. Back in my room I look around one more time and remember the Christmas money I've got in my box—a couple of twenties—so I grab them, and my water bottle, and my coat. Then I turn to the door, and there's Bea. School must be out. She says, "What are you doing?"

"Leaving."

"Running away?"

"I guess if you want to call it that."

"Oh." We're both quiet for a bunch of seconds. Then, "You'll die, you know."

"Did you hear Mom a minute ago? I'll die if I stay, too."

"I didn't hear. I just got home. But one is for sure and the other is only maybe."

"None of this has ever happened before. They don't know. And one is me deciding, and the other is me in a petri dish."

She turns her face away, and I don't have enough nice left to say anything to make her feel better. She looks back at me again. "I think it's a bad idea."

"You gonna stop me?"

Another bunch of seconds. "No."

"You gonna tell on me?"

She opens her mouth and stands there like that. I start toward the door. Her eyes go shiny and she says, "Felix, don't."

My eyes are as dry as a rock in the Mojave Desert. Red and black, black and red, swirling. "I have to."

Now her eyes are full of tears. She makes a little fist and does the world's softest punch on my shoulder and turns away. "Then, I guess . . . bye," she mumbles at the wall.

That almost gets me. Almost, but not quite. I touch her back with one fingertip. "Yeah, OK, Be-have. Bye," I say, and I go downstairs.

Mom and Rick are in the kitchen, and their voices are sharper now. I hear Rick say, ". . . you and Ursula . . ." so I know they're not fighting just about my glorious chess future anymore. The dining room is empty, but Rick's tablet is there on the table, charging, so I unplug the charger and shove it and the tablet into my duffel. I also grab two apples from the fruit bowl. Then I stealth-walk to the side door and ease my way out, making sure the screen doesn't slam behind me, and start walking down the sidewalk away from the kitchen window. Mr. Jeffries is in his yard, digging in a flower bed. He waves at me and I nod back. Then I turn the corner and the house is out of sight.

I have no idea where I'm going and this tornado of feels is spinning inside me, what with the red and the black still, plus the joy of breaking free, and then this horrible wrench-at-the-heart thing, like, "MMOMMMMYYYYY!!!!" But when I get down to Lincoln Street, where I could turn left toward town or right toward the railroad tracks, I turn right. And when I hear the whistle, I start to run.

I've loved trains ever since I was little. I've always dreamed about what it would be like to jump on a passing train and get whisked away to some new, different future. I have this stupid literal imagination, so usually the future I make up fills with trouble pretty quickly, but still, when I hear the whistle and imagine leaping into a boxcar door, whatever knot I am tied in at that particular moment loosens a bit.

Well, this time I really do it, except for the boxcar part, on account of all the boxcar doors being closed. I get to the crossing just as the locomotive comes into view around the curve. Not going fast yet—still getting up to speed out of the yard. The gate is down and a couple of cars are waiting, so I cross the street behind them with my hand hiding my face in case it's anyone who knows me, and then I cross the ditch and angle back into the woods between the road and the tracks. I make it to the edge of the trees just as the locomotive looms up in all its thunder and smoke, and I hold back for a second so the engineer won't see me, then step out crunch crunch on the big gravel and watch the cars going by, rattle rattle bang bang. Lots of oil tankers go by—no good—and then boxcars with their doors closed. I can see the end of the train coming, but there's a flatcar with nothing on it, so I toss the duffel up first and hear something crack (the tablet screen, but it still works), and then I leap as best I can—stupid creaky Pose, but I make it—and scrabble up.

And so now here I am, sitting with my back against the little front wall of the car so I'm out of the wind and out of sight of the locomotive, watching the scenery slip back behind. I've got the tablet on my knees, typing this. The train is still picking up speed, and soon it will get dark. And then what? Stupid literal imagination says discomfort, hunger, danger—but you know what, screw it. I'm free.

4 Days to Go

Things I would have brought if I had thought of them: more and warmer clothes, more food, a sleeping bag, and toilet paper. Live and learn, I guess. Ha ha funny, live and learn.

What's really weird is having the tablet, because even though I'm currently lying on a car seat under a bridge, I still know exactly what time it is (6:13 am) and I can check my regulars and post to my secret blog. I was smart—I found the settings for location controls and turned them off, and I haven't done anything where people could track me.

I don't know what to do. If I go back I am going to be in such trouble, and of course all the things I wrote yesterday are still true, but on the other hand I am sick of being attached to this . . . this . . . hyperdimensional freak. No offense, Zyx.

offense question mark

Nothing ever bothers you, does it? Can I insult you? Is it possible?

insult question mark

Yeah, I know from other times—I can't. Well, screw you. I hate you.

not hate love

Yep. Whatever.

So back to yesterday. Where was I? On the train, right. Well, after that last entry, the sun begins to go down and the train speeds up, and the wind starts whipping so hard it makes my hair sting my face around my eyes. Also, my mouth gets dry really fast. I thought I was so clever, bringing my water bottle, but I drink half of it in the first hour before stopping to save some. Then even though my mouth is still dry I start to need to pee, which, how are you supposed to do that on a speeding train? Then I get scared and want to go back home, but the train is going too fast to jump, and it's already too far to walk back. So I pull out all the clothes

I brought and put them on. The sun sinks behind clouds and the sky turns red.

I start to wonder how far the train is going. I know we are headed south, so straight into Boston? Or stop in Portland? I hope not Boston. I start to get all worked up about maybe going around Boston too, straight to New York or, gah, Georgia or something. How far do trains go before they have to stop for gas or fuel or whatever? I have no idea.

Just when I start to panic, the train slows down again, and I see that we are pulling into Portland. I recognize the bridge and the buildings on the hill behind it from all the times we've driven in. The train keeps slowing and pretty soon I think that if there is a soft space maybe I could jump, so I wrap the tablet in the middle of all the clothes I can bear to take off again—by now it's getting really chilly—and then climb down to the bottom rung of the ladder on the side of the car and watch for a good moment to jump. My duffel keeps banging my legs and I think, Next time, backpack. Next time. Ha ha ha.

Well, who knows?

Look at that: a little spurt of hope. Not rational, but I'll take it.

Anyway, the train is going around a curve, so I can see it all laid out in front of me, and suddenly way up at the front I see a man's face sticking out of the locomotive window, looking back at me. My heart spurts up into my throat and I see a patch of ground coming with more grass than rocks, so I toss-drop the duffel and leap out and land running for about two steps and stumble and do a somersault and end up on my back, looking up at the sky. The train continues to roll by, CLANK CLANK clank clank (clank clank), and then the silence is big in my ears after all the wind and noise. My elbow hurts—I think I must have whacked it on a rock—but other than that I'm not injured.

So I fetch the duffel and start walking along the tracks. There's a river or bay on the left with lots of oil tanks on the other shore, and on the right a steep hill covered with scrubby trees and bushes, with houses on top. Most of the houses have lights on—by this time it's getting really gray. There's a road too, down by the water, with more lights, but I stay on the far side of the tracks from that. And there's a big bridge ahead, and under the bridge the rock of the hill kinda scoops back in, so there's a little cavelike place.

As I get closer to the bridge I see there's a moldy old armchair sitting out at the edge of the trees, and behind it a couple of paths going back through the bushes. I follow one over a little rise and find a clearing. Nobody's around. There's a place where fire has made rocks black, and there's a bunch of beer cans and broken glass all around, and I have started to breathe through my nose because there's a porta potty smell in the air. In fact, I can see some . . . well, you know, lying right out on the ground. Yuck. There are also a couple of logs for sitting on, a bunch of graffiti on the rocks, and there's a mattress partially pulled apart and sorta shoved back in the bushes, which I might lie down on if it was a choice between that and, say, getting struck by lightning.

Then I hear a stick snap and up on the hill I see a guy with his hair sticking out all shaggy under the bottom of his bill cap. He's coming down through the trees, going sideways to me, and I'm pretty sure he doesn't see me, but I still sneak back as fast as I can over the little rise and head in the opposite direction, toward the cave under the bridge.

It's almost completely dark by this time, and a cold damp-feeling wind has come up. More clouds are filling the sky. A flashlight is another thing I didn't think of bringing, so I grope my way back in the dark-gray light. There's a lot of trash in the weeds, but it doesn't stink like the fire-pit place, and toward the back I find a big old wide car seat. It has holes picked in it and stuff, but the plasticky cover is pretty clean-looking, so I sit down. I'm hungry, so I eat one of my apples with a swallow of water, and think about going up and trying to buy some food, but then I think of cops and trying to find this place again in the dark and I don't go. Then there's nothing left to do but wonder about what's going on at home. Mom all upset, I figure, and Bea probably in trouble unless she lied about seeing me leave, and maybe even Grandy getting worked up. And I feel bad and stupid and lost and helpless.

Also, tired. Soon it's completely dark except for the low gray glow from the clouds outside—gray with a tinge of city-light yellow. I can't think of anything else to do except try to sleep, so I figure out a way I can sort of lean half-sideways on the seat without falling off when I relax into the Pose, and after a while I actually start to get sleepy. Then the seat tips and almost dumps me, so I get up again and stick a rock underneath it. Then I thrash around for a long time until finally, believe it or not, I fall asleep.

I have no idea what time it is when cold water on my face wakes me. The gray outside is darker now—I guess most of the city has gone to bed—and it's raining. The wind is gusting in and spraying drops across my face. Not all the time, only the really big gusts. I'm shivering. I get up and try to drag the seat farther in under the overhang, but it's too heavy. I do manage to pull it around partway so the back is to the wind, which maybe helps a little. I also manage to put one of the runners down on the toe of my sneaker, which hurts like hell, but eventually I get the thing stable again, and after a while I drift back to sleep.

When I woke up again just a little while ago it was still dark and still raining, but the dark was slightly lighter, so I figured somewhere up above the clouds the sun was beginning to come up. The rain and wind have both gotten less, so no more splashes of drops. That doesn't mean I am comfortable, though. What woke me up was the cold. My teeth aren't chattering, but only because my jaw muscles have basically seized shut, and the rest of me isn't so much shivering as having little convulsions. And pushing against the Pose feels nearly as hard as it was on that lockup morning. It hurts bad.

So what do I do now? I'm hungry and thirsty and I need to pee. And that last one was easy to take care of, but no fun in the cold. And now I just drank my last swallow of water and ate my last apple, even the gristly part around the seeds, but it just made me hungrier.

Zyx, I apologize.

apologize question mark

Don't you get it? I ran away. That means no Procedure. It means we're stuck together forever, or until the end anyway. But if I go back . . . No, I can't face that. There's no right answer. What do you do when there's no right answer?

no answer only be do now all right

But I'm not deciding just for me. I've decided for you. You're stuck with my decision.

not stuck

Yes, you are. We're stuck together. That's the whole point.

zyx love felix

Stop saying that! It only makes it worse!

zyx love felix

Stop it! How can I . . . Wait, someone's coming. Better hide the tablet.

Still 4 Days to Go

Now it's night again, and I have to explain everything that has happened today.

I was afraid the person coming might be hat-hair guy, but it wasn't. Actually I thought the person was a girl, because of the long hair, which was all I could see at first, but then he gets a little closer and I see it's a guy, and he looks young. Not a teenager anymore, but not much older. He's wearing skinny-leg jeans and a leather jacket with fringe on it, beat-up hiking boots, and a backpack with the straps scrunching the jacket into bunches. He stops a few feet away.

He doesn't look dangerous. He doesn't look dirty or homeless, either. Just a guy you might pass on the street and not notice. We look at each other for a minute and then he says, "Hey, little brother." His voice is soft, and he kinda looks sideways at you and then away when he talks. Shy, though, is what it says, not shifty. He reminds me of Ash.

I don't say anything. I just sit there with my heartbeat shaking me back and forth a little.

"My train isn't going to be by for a bit yet. Mind if I sit down?" He waves a hand at the weeds and rocks around us, like, Dude, you're hogging the only seat.

I still can't talk, but I shift over and hunch myself up. He drops his pack and flops onto the seat, letting his head roll on the back, sticking his skinny legs out in front of him. "Thanks," he says. Then he says, "I think maybe the rain is going to stop soon. I hope so. It is seriously unfun catching out in a downpour." Then we sit in silence. I'm so hungry my stomach hurts, and I feel shaky and weak. I think again about climbing up into the town and trying to find a grocery store, and my stomach makes a noise like some undersea creature crying in pain. It actually sounds out loud in the stillness.

The guy glances at me, then pulls his pack around and opens a drawstring and takes out one of those sandwiches inside a triangle of clear plastic like they sell in gas stations. When I see it my stomach makes another noise and all of a sudden my mouth is full of water, but it comes into my head that he must have stolen it, and I get panicky. Could I be arrested for eating stolen food?

He pops the lid, pulls out one of the matching wedges, and holds it out to me. "You want something to eat?" he says. I catch a whiff of chicken salad and my hand moves by itself, but I pull it back again because I've still got the panic going, and I say something stupid, like, "Is it . . . I mean, did you . . . uh uh duh duh . . ." He looks at me, puzzled but not upset, and I feel ashamed, so I change my question. "Are you sure?" I say. "Half a sandwich isn't very much." Meaning, the half that's left for him.

"Oh, no worries," he says, "there's plenty more where that came from," and he tips the pack so I can see what looks like a chip bag and the edge of some kind of box and a bottle top. This does not answer the question of stolen versus bought, but I don't care anymore. I take the sandwich half and bite so far into it that it paints mayonnaise on both my cheeks, and then I gobble the whole thing in about ten seconds.

"Hungry," he says. "I know how it feels."

"Thanks," I say. My voice comes out thick, from the mayo. I would really like to eat the other half of the sandwich too, but I don't dare say anything about that.

"No worries." More silence. Then, "So, what's your name, little brother?"

"Felix."

"You can call me Malcolm," he says. "'Cause that's my name." He smiles a little. I'm starting to feel more relaxed, and pretty soon, sitting there with the light getting warmer—there's a touch of gold now—I ask the question that's on my mind. "So, you're here to catch a train?"

"That's right. Should be by in half an hour or so."

"What's it like?"

"Riding the rails? It's totally gnarly." I want to know more, but I'm not sure I'm allowed to ask. After a second, though, he goes on by himself. He talks about the proper way to jump onto and off of a train, and about wearing dark clothes so the bulls won't see you—the bulls, he says, are the railroad police—and about how an open boxcar is great if you can find it, but that's kind of a romantic notion really because usually it's flatcars or other kinds with platforms on the end, and the only kind that's really no good to ride is the tank cars. He talks slowly with pauses between, and smiles to himself and shakes his head, like he's listening to himself along with me. "Gnarly," he says again, and then there is a long silence. Then he says, "What about you, little brother? Where are you headed?"

That mixes me up, and I go to talk a couple times but stop again. He glances at me through his hair, hanging forward and loose. "You're pretty young-looking to be out on your own," he says. "Whadja do, run away from home?"

Asking it right out like that makes it easy to answer. "Yeah."

He nods and does the fish-lips thing that people do when they're agreeing. "That's cool," he says. "Man's gotta do what a man's gotta do."

Him calling me a man like that makes me feel about seven years old, and all of a sudden I want more than anything in the world to see my mom's face. He says, "None of my business, but where's home?"

"Littlefield."

"Not far, then. Just up the line." He doesn't say, So you could get back easily if you wanted to, but I think it, and then I start twitching, because I can only imagine how profoundly squirm-worthy it would be to go back. Malcolm is staring at his boots, which he's flopping back and forth in the dirt. If he has noticed how I talk and move, I can't tell. He says, "Well, you're welcome to catch on with me, if you want, when my train comes."

"No thanks," I say, and now we both know that I don't want to go any farther.

"That's cool," he says again. More silence. "This is a pretty nasty place to stay, though," he finally goes on. "Even if the sun does come out." He seems to make up his mind. "Listen," he says, sitting up and looking right at me for once. "I know a house with some good people in it, if you, you know . . . need a place to stay."

I don't say no this time, so I guess I must think it's an OK idea. Strangers. Scary stranger yesterday. Nice stranger today. I feel like there are a whole bunch of rules for life that I didn't even know existed yesterday. What's the rule about nice people tell-ing you other people are nice? Do you believe them? Again I talk without knowing what I'm going to say. "How would I find it?"

"Oh, I'll walk you up there, if you like. It's not far."

"But, your train."

"No worries. There will be another one tomorrow."

I don't want to make this guy miss his train, but my feet are so cold, and my stomach is twisting around like that little sandwich only made it mad. And he's right about where we are—it's a wet chilly hole in a cliff with a bunch of trash and a car seat in it. No place to live, even for a little while. "OK, thanks," I say.

"Cool," he says, and pushes himself to his feet. He picks up his pack and puts it on. I get up too, bent-kneed at first because of the cold and the Pose, and gather my stuff. Then he starts picking his way through the weeds toward the light, which is getting strong now, and I follow. When we get out under the sky, I see there are patches of blue. The air tastes cool and soft. It's a fresh morning. Malcolm gives me a nod, and we start hiking up toward the city of Portland, Maine.

The streets when we reach them are quiet house streets, not busy business streets. First we pass through a couple of blocks of big houses with large clear windows where the lawns are clipped and the garages are freshly painted and there are nice shiny new cars in them. Then we pass a school and a building that looks like it might have offices in it. A block down a side street there's a storefront with some neon that my stomach makes me turn toward, but Malcolm says, "We can get some breakfast at the house, if you want," so we go on.

After the business street the houses look older and less well cared for. They are also a lot closer together, so there's less room for flower beds and stuff, just skinny side yards mostly covered in asphalt with two or three cars crammed in, or little weedy patches. It's one of these houses he stops at. It's set back a little from the street, with a tiny double weed-patch front yard and concrete steps going up. I stop at the bottom of the stairs and think for a second about running off down the street, but he says, "Come on," and I do.

The door from the street opens into a bare little room, not even a room really, just a place with a couple of closed doors, a couple of bicycles, and a hall that goes back to another closed door at the end. It's open overhead, though, with the stairs wrapping around, and every little sound echoes up into the space. The stairs are so old that all the places people touch when they climb are dark and shiny. We go up with our footsteps echoing, past a little square window with colored glass in it, to a landing and another door.

Malcolm puts his finger to his lips. "It's still early," he whispers. "They're all going to be asleep. But welcome to the House on Harmony Street." Was that the street name? I didn't notice. I give him a look, and he whispers, "Because everyone who lives here always gets along so well," and I totally can't tell if he's being sarcastic or not. We go in.

Bare floors. Not much furniture at all. Someone has been drawing pictures on the walls with crayons, which now that I type it looks like I mean a knee-level scrawl of a little house with curly smoke and a tree and birds drawn by some rug rat, but that's not what I mean at all. On one wall there's a life-size unicorn—I mean, life-size if unicorns are the same size as horses—and it's done in a bunch of different colors and it's wicked cool. Malcolm sees me looking and murmurs, "Nice, huh? Lauren did that."

A skinny black-except-for-white-face-patches cat runs up and wraps itself around my leg, purring, and Malcolm whispers, "Still hungry? No doubt there's a ton of spaghetti left over from last night."

Something in me just lets go, finally, and I follow him into the kitchen, thinking, Whatever happens happens. One corner of the kitchen is higher than the other. There are a couple sick-looking plants in the window, more art on the walls, and a sink full of dishes with stuff caked on them. Malcolm opens the fridge and pulls out a white bowl with a plastic bag over the top. It has a big wad of spaghetti noodles in it with sauce and cheese bits on them. He gets two forks out of a drawer and we both start taking bites, standing there in the middle of the kitchen with him holding the bowl.

While we're still eating I hear a door and footsteps and a girl comes in. She's got straight red hair that's cut so it comes down to points in front, and the red is so dark and bright at the same time that I figure her real hair color is more like her eyebrows, which are brown. It's really cute, though. She's cute. She's like Malcolm in age—early twenties. She's wearing nice clothes, which surprises me at first, because I figure, Saturday morning, pajamas or whatever, but then it's clear from the talk that she's on her way to her job, which is some restaurant thing. She shows no surprise at seeing Malcolm and me there, just says, "Hey," and goes past us to the fridge to get juice. Once she has it she leans against the counter and says, "So, stranger, what's your name?"

"Felix," I say, through a mouthful of noodles.

"Hey, Felix. I'm Lauren."

I swallow. "You drew the unicorn."

"Yeah."

"Awesome unicorn."

She tips her head and smiles, and when she smiles she gets a whadayacall, a dimple, at the corner of her mouth, and also her eyes light up, and I think, Wow, if I liked girls.

Once my stomach is full—I have a glass of water from the sink too—I start yawning like crazy. Malcolm tells Lauren, without going into details, that I had a rough night, and she says, "You can crash on the couch if you like," and then she's gone to work, and all of a sudden there's nothing I want to do more than lie down on something soft and warm and clean. So I do. I kick my shoes off and scrunch into the corner of the couch, which seems good for the Pose, and the cat comes running over and curls up on my stomach, purring, and the vibration of the purr and the warmth of its furry body spread through my whole body and I'm out.

. . . .

When I wake up again, I figure from the stiffness and pain and the flat taste in my mouth that I have been asleep for a while—maybe a couple of hours. The cat is gone and the room is empty, but I can hear someone making noises in the kitchen. I get up kinda slow, trying not to make a sound, but I guess I do anyway, because I hear footsteps and then a new person comes in from the kitchen.

This new person is short and sorta round around the edges, and I feel a little squirt of squirminess, because I can't tell right away if I'm looking at a male or a female person. Whoever it is has a nice face, though, with a smile and chubby cheeks and eyebrows up like, Hey, what's going on? The cheeks are part of what's throwing me off. Along with the rounded edges they say girl, but the clothes and the little bit of hair on the face say boy. So I think to myself, When vo speaks, I'll know, but it doesn't work out that way. "Hey," vo says, in a medium-high, slightly scratchy voice that could totally go either way. "You doin' OK?"

"Uh . . . yeah, thanks."

"Malcolm told me you're a friend of his. You guys known each other long?"

My first impulse is to lie, but vo is smiling so nicely, and also, I still have the feeling of whatever happens happens, so I say, "Oh, you know, about . . . What time is it?"

"Almost noon."

"About six hours."

Vo snorts. "I thought maybe. What's your name?"

"Felix." And I'm thinking, OK, a name, now I'll know.

"Hey, Felix. I'm Cam. Welcome to the House on Harmony Street."

Cam. Gah. But, you know, living with Grandy, I've learned that, girl, boy, it doesn't matter, so I just say, "Thanks."

Cam seems to think for a second, looking at me, then starts to say, "You're awfully young, aren't you . . ." but at this point one of the other doors opens and a new guy stumbles out, wearing nothing but boxer shorts. It's dark in the room behind him, like if there's a window, the shade is down. His hair is rumpled and his eyes are still mostly closed. Cam does introductions, and Steven, is his name, shuffles into the bathroom. Then Cam asks if I'm hungry, and I say, yes, I am, so I follow ven into the kitchen, and vo sets us both up with cheese sandwiches and juice. There's a little table with a chair and a stool, so we sit at that to eat, and

Cam talks about veir work, which is some kind of extreme cleaning job, getting into the crawl spaces under houses and stuff.

After a bit Steven comes in, dressed and looking more awake, and makes food for himself. He enters into the conversation, and one of the first things he says is, So, what do you play? Which catches me off guard, so I stare at him, and he says, Music, what instrument do you play? Like, everyone should. So I say, Guitar, a little, wondering when is the last time I actually touched it. That's cool, he says, so like, folk, rock, classical, jazz? Rock, I guess, I say. That's cool, he says again, but you do need to check out jazz, and immediately he goes into his room and comes back out with a saxophone. He plays a little run, to warm up, I guess, and then he starts tapping his foot and closes his eyes and kinda curls his body around the saxophone and plays this jumpy funky song, and when he gets to the end he goes back in and changes it all around and makes it amazing, and I can tell Zyx likes it too, because I start twitching and flailing *jazz pretty*

Yeah, jazz pretty. You've been awfully quiet today, I suddenly notice.

yes quiet watch listen be

Right. You still don't get it, do you? If I don't go back, we're both gonna die. Or at least I am, and if you're not, you're going to be melded with a dead human, which, yuck. Although, maybe that's where zombies come from.

die not die all same jazz chess sing dance pretty now now now

Yeah, could you put a lid on it, please? I've got some story left to tell here. After that, I tell you what, I'll let you type whatever you want. OK? We've never done that before. I'll just sit back and empty my mind and give you my hands, and you can type whatever you want.

yes

OK, thanks. You gonna be quiet now?

. . .

OK.

Anyway, by now I'm feeling really safe with these people, so when Cam starts asking me questions I answer them, and pretty soon vo knows how old I am and where I live, and then vo says, "Malcolm said you ran away."

"Uh-huh, yeah, I did."

"Things bad at home?"

I drop my eyes and start twisting and twitching. Sometimes that's not Zyx, sometimes it's just me being me.

"Who you got at home?"

That's easier. "My sister, Bea, and my mom, and Grandy."

"Grandy?" says Steven.

"Uh, my grandparent . . . vo switches back and forth between—"

" 'Vo'?"

"Uh, yeah, that's a word Grandy made up . . . a pronoun, right? For when you don't know whether someone is, uh . . . male or female . . . like you," I say, looking at Cam, and then I realize what I've said and my face goes hot and I drop my eyes again.

There's a little silence, and then Steven and Cam both laugh— nice laughs, though. Cam says, "Kid, you're all right. Vo, huh?

I've never heard that one before. But I do use he and him. I'm trans. You know, identified as female at birth, but—"

"Oh. OK," I say, and Cam nods with approval, like I just scored a point by being cool about that. But it's easy, 'cause of Grandy.

Then I'm kinda hoping Cam has forgotten what he (I can say now) was asking, but he hasn't. "So, Bea and Mom and Grandy," he says. "You guys get along OK?"

Well, that makes me want to cry. In fact, I want to cry so bad, I do. One burst of a sob, and then quieter tears that I can't hold back.

"Dude," says Steven, and when I look at him, his face is all sad. "It's hard to know what to do."

Cam puts his hand on mine. It's a small hand, but I don't think of it like a girl hand now. "You miss them," he says.

"Yeah."

"Got my cell in my room. Wanna make a call?"

It's the same question I've been asking myself, and what I

realize is, Yeah, I would like to call, except I don't want to have to explain myself. What I really want to do is go back. I have to go back. So what I say to Cam is, no thanks, I don't want to call, but I do want to go home.

Then there's this dumb confused bit about transportation, because I guess nobody in the house owns a car and they feel bad because they can't instantly drive me back to my doorstep. They're talking about pitching in to buy me a bus ticket and I'm sitting there feeling like a little kid being talked about by his parents while he's there in the room, and I realize something obvious—they think I don't have any money—so I pull out the two twenties and Steven stops in the middle of a sentence and says, "Well, jeez, kid, why didn't you say so?" Then there's some quick research on a phone and we find out that there's one bus a day back to Littlefield, but it has already left for today. Then Cam says I can stay on the couch again until morning, and I almost cry again.

Then I just hang out for the rest of the day. Steven invites me into his room and plays me some jazz on records, real records, big black disks, and Zyx and I both like it, but nobody says anything about the flailing. Then Lauren comes home and there's pizza, which they won't let me help pay for. Then Steven goes to play a "gig," and this other girl Sarah comes by and Lauren goes out with her, and then Cam and I hang out, watching TV for a while, and they're all just really nice people, but I want my mom.

So now it's gotten late and the house is quiet. Cam is in his room with the door closed, and I'm lying here thinking about tomorrow. I still know I want to go home, but I don't know yet what I'm going to do when I get there. But I guess whatever happens happens. This couch is soft and warm, and really OK for the Pose. I think I could sleep.

....

Awake again.

House quiet. Street quiet. Dark except for light from street-light.

Something woke me. Not something outside, though. Something inside. Zyx, this feeling I have of . . . I can't describe . . . Is it you?

yes

I feel like I'm being pulled in a direction I don't understand. What are you doing?

show

What do you mean?

felix say let type but better show life in four never before fear but love more show gift

Um, do I understand right? You want to show me what it's like where you live?

yes

But, what's the fear part?

fear hurt felix not fear more safe

You were afraid it would hurt me, so you didn't do it.

yes

And now somehow you know it is safe? How do you know?

know because done ago

You already did it? You took me there?

yes

When!?

small ago felix sleep

While I was asleep just now. You took me.

yes

You risked my life?

yes small risk

But still!

felix live

Yes, I'm still alive. And I should be mad. But I'm not. Wow, it's quiet. I can hear my heart beating. It's the loudest sound in the room. In the whole world, feels like. No, not mad. Just . . . stranger than I have ever felt.

question mark

You want to know what I want to do.

yes

All right, then. I don't care if it's not safe. I want to know. I've always been curious what it's like where you are. So, how do we do this?

must breathe slow hold still empty mind let open let carry let bring

All right, I'm doing it. I'm going to keep typing as long as i can and what is that like light like air like opening of each part of me into every part of me am felix am zyx am all such light such space such light so fast so still such light three is one is three is one

3 Days to Go

And now it is morning. Full sunlight morning, I mean, though it's still early and the house is quiet. I'm feeling all safe and warm in the nest of blankets and pillows that Cam and Steven and Lauren made for me. They have been so nice to me. I'm a total stranger, and they took me in and fed me and gave me a place to sleep, and Cam is going to walk me to the bus station in time to catch the bus back to Littlefield. It's so strange, being alive in the world. I'm glad I'm alive, but it's so strange.

Zyx, are you there?

yes

Do you want to say anything?

. . .

Well then, I want to try to describe what happened last night, or earlier this morning, when I woke up and let Zyx . . . um . . . do whatever vo did. A field trip to the fourth dimension, I guess.

How to start. Hm.

All right, maybe like this. I used to think about how if I got accidentally merged with some poor two-dimensional creature, I'd have to be careful not to pull it out of its plane into our world, because it would have no thickness. All its insides would be outsides in our space, and I figured it would just fall apart like wet tissue paper. Zyx, would it have maybe been like that for me in your space?

maybe but not

So that was the risk. But you tried, maybe just a tiny bit, I hope, and it was OK.

yes

OK. I guess. I'm still alive, so OK.

So what I felt last night was, Zyx pulled me in a direction I didn't understand, and it was like every atom I'm made of was growing larger (unless it was smaller) at the same time, but somehow without them squishing each other (or pulling apart). And it kept happening until each atom got so incredibly huge—unless it was so incredibly tiny—that the border between the edges of me and the beginning of everything else went away. And then . . . um . . . this is where words really start to seem less useful. . . .

I'll try another way. I sort of got the idea . . . or *was* the idea . . . that there is this one thing that Is . . . an either impossibly small or impossibly large thing—let's say small, just to say something . . . a zero-dimensional point, and everything that exists is in this point . . . No, that's not right either.

OK, try this. This zero-dimensional point of Is, it's flying all around space in this incredibly complex pattern, faster than light, faster than thought, and everything that exists is the afterimage of the path it flies, which is like a spiral made of spirals nested in spirals going infinitely down and infinitely up, and then everything that exists is the impossibly beautiful dance of the one Is particle . . . unless Is is the space it's dancing in. Nelson, this is hard.

One more try. The one and three thing. There was the one Is, which was either everything or the zero-dimensional-point thing, and then there was the three that was the one Is and the Is Not that it danced through and then the difference between them, and, you know what? I'm done. I can't explain. But things seem different now.

And, here's a chat window. I thought I turned that off. Um, it's Hector.

H: Felix?

F: Yeah, I'm here.

H: How u doin?

F: OK. Which is a way too simple way to say, my life is incredibly strange and scary right now. But, OK.

H: Ok

H: Hey Felix?

F: Yeah?

H: It's Ok about calling me stupid

F: OK, thanks. I'm really sorry about that.

H: I just get so tired of people seeing me as less than them

F: Yeah. I know what you mean. So again, sorry.

H: Ok

H: You there?

F: Yeah, I'm here. I was just wondering if you know anything about, uh, well . . .

H: About what?

F: Well, let's just say, I'm not at home right now.

H: ?

F: I jumped a train. Yesterday. I mean, two days ago now.

H: o.O

F: Yeah.

H: Why?

F: It's hard to explain. Or, no it's not. I freaked about the Procedure. You remember I told you about that.

H: Yah

F: I heard my mom say something about how my chances of surviving were lower than she said before, so I ran. Also, there's some stuff about it that you don't know.

H: Private stuff

F: Yeah, I guess. Or just so strange I don't think you'd believe me. But I'm not supposed to tell.

H: It's cool

H: So where are you?

F: In a house in Portland. The House on Harmony Street, they call it. A guy I met gave me food and showed me where this place is and the people are really nice.

H: No way!

F: Yeah, it does seem unusual now that I think about it.

H: That is all so awesome

F: Uh, thanks, I think.

H: I'm not being sarcastic. It's truly awesome

F: OK, thanks I'm sure. :-)

H: :)

H: You there?

F: Yeah. Thinking.

H: What are you going to do?

F: That's what I'm thinking about. I know the next part. I'm getting a bus back to Littlefield this morning. It's what comes after that I don't know. I feel bad about what I did, and I'm not sure how to handle going home.

F: You there?

H: Yah. Felix, I have a question

F: What?

H: Would you like it if . . . I mean . . .

F: ?

H: I could come meet your bus. If you want

H: You there?

F: Really? You would do that?

H: Yah. You want me to?

F: Yes!

H: Really?

F: Really.

H: Really???

F: Yeah.

H: Cool. Bus from Portland. See you there

F: You're leaving?

F: Hector?

F: Uh . . . bye. See you.

Still 3 Days to Go

The House on Harmony Street started to wake up just after I chatted with Hector. Steven and Cam got up at the same time and did this funny thing at the door to the bathroom—No no no, after *you* my dear Alphonse—and they fed me English muffins with peanut butter for breakfast and still wouldn't take any of my money. Lauren wasn't around but that other girl Sarah was, and she had a whole bunch of blond hair streaked with darker streaks and was walking around barefoot in nothing but a cotton T-shirt, and I had to be careful about where I pointed my eyes because I didn't want to be a jerk.

They let me use the shower, and I brushed my teeth and put on the other set of clothes I brought and felt practically normal, except for the coil of something deep down in the bottom of my stomach. Fear, I guess. But my brain was also still full of the Experience Zyx had given me, so, coils and roils, but I let them happen and kept moving.

Then Cam walks me to the bus station through an almost warm sunny morning—I guess it's actually finally spring. He's such a nice guy. He smiles a lot, which is creepy in some people, like you wonder what they're really up to behind that fakey mask, but with Cam it's just like he's happy all the time. On the way he talks and jokes and gets me laughing, and that helps, because as we enter the bus station and I buy my ticket, the coils and roils ratchet up. Oh, and the change from my ticket is about seven bucks and when I hold it out to Cam and say awkwardly, "For the pizza and stuff," he gives me this look like I've insulted him, so I shut up and put it away.

Cam hangs with me until the bus pulls up with its hiss of brakes, hiss of doors opening. All I have is my duffel, so I don't have to stand in the line for putting luggage underneath. I just climb up the steps after giving my ticket to the bus driver. The driver doesn't hiss—he mumbles.

The bus trip is like being trapped inside a can of air freshener. I ignore the little TVs and watch out the window, which I wish wasn't tinted. I'm on the left side, so mostly I watch other cars on the turnpike, wondering where they're going. I'm headed home and maybe going to my death, but maybe to the rest of my life, too. And these people, they're also all headed toward their deaths or their lives. Each second that goes by, we're all one second closer to the rest of our lives and our deaths. I wouldn't call that exactly comforting, but it helps me feel less alone.

When we get off the Littlefield exit, the coils and roils really start to work out down there in my intestines, and I know this is not about death or life or about what the hell am I going to say to my mom. It's only, Will Hector be there? And what will happen?

He's there, standing by a post. He's wearing jeans and a white T-shirt and dark glasses, and his face looks closed up. For one second I think about staying on the bus, but then only one other person gets up to get out, and I jump up and clump clump down the stairs and walk over to him.

He puts his dark glasses up on his head, and his face doesn't look closed anymore. Now it has in it all the things I have seen in him, all at once, little bits of how he can be funny and quiet and mad and happy. . . . Breathe, Felix! Yeah. So we stand there for a second, looking at each other, and then he gives me this awkward bro hug, shoulder to shoulder, which I give back as much as I can with the duffel knocking around our knees. The cinnamon smell of his hair, plus something more complicated I don't have a name for, goes straight up through my nose and into my brain. "Hey," he says, which is good, because without help I would not be able to speak. "Hey," I say. And then we turn and start walking toward the neighborhood where we both live.

It's nice, just walking. I shift the duffel in case by some wild chance he wants to hold hands, which even with all these people around I wish he would, but he doesn't do anything, and I don't have the nerve to take his hand myself.

So now I need to explain that in this part of Littlefield there's a tree-filled place, and a corner of it lies between the bus station and our neighborhood. Hector's house is farther, so we're going to get to my house first, but to get to either house we either have to go around the Woods, as they are called, or cut through them. There's a fence but it has loose places, and anyone who grew up close by knows veir way around the paths inside. There's a fire ring and a couple of secret fort places, and another place where people have made little huts and lean-tos out of sticks, so it's like a village of forest gnomes or something. And there's one longer path that loops back and passes through a stand of tall pine trees, and right in the middle of that, you can almost feel like you're far away from any houses or gas stations or schools or whatever. A little patch of wilderness.

We come to the first loose place in the fence and we don't even have to talk about it. I hold the fence for Hector to squeeze through, and then he pushes with his foot so I can squeeze through, and still without talking about it we take the turn that leads to the deep path. Pretty soon the loudest sounds are wind and birds. I hear blue jays making a racket, and other birds Grandy hasn't taught me yet twittering up high where I can't see them. Then Hector says, "Um . . ."

We walk a little farther, and I say, "Um . . . what?"

"You said there was something else. Something I wouldn't believe."

We stop walking and I turn to face him. I can feel myself making a bunch of different faces that go along with the confusion in my head, but I don't manage to get as far as words, and after a couple of seconds he says, "You can trust me?" It's funny how he says it, like it's both a statement and a question. He doesn't look away, and I make myself not look away too. We're right in the pines now. The breeze is shushing in the needles, and I have all these feels, feels with wheels, coiling and roiling. It's like the spirals within spirals of the Experience Zyx gave me. The silence stretches out, and just when I'm starting to feel awkward he puts his head over on one side and says, "Felix, do you know what a trust walk is?"

"No."

"It's a thing I learned in camp." His eyes flicker away for a second, but then they come back. "What you do is, one person closes his eyes, and the other person holds his hand and then they walk together, and the other person has to guide the one who has his eyes closed." His face is all serious when he's saying this, but then he does this shrug/smile that makes me want to hug him. "You wanna try?"

"OK." I know he means, me close my eyes, so standing there under the tall pines I close my eyes and I feel him take my hand—his hand is warm and solid in mine—and then he pulls gently, and I take a step and another, and we're walking. He's leading me and I'm trusting him, not exactly following, but letting myself be led, side by side.

He doesn't say anything except about the walking, like, "Be careful, there's a root here," and "Now we're turning to the right," and I don't say anything at all, because I'm totally caught up in smelling and feeling the air, and listening to the space around me, and feeling how birds are flying through it in beautiful curving lines. Then I think about the pine needles and the budding twigs on the trees and how they're connected to branches connected to the big gnarled trunks plunging down into the ground, and then the roots exploding out again like mirror-image branches, all the way out to the tiny rootlets right under our walking feet, and that gets me thinking about spirals again, and then I think about how the spirals that I feel inside me seem to be reaching out toward the spirals that I can feel spinning around inside Hector, and his hand is talking to me through mine, pulling, moving, a thing of its own not connected to me, but at the same time we're touching and connected and twined together by all the pullings and pushings and little twistings . . . pull push closer farther, together apart together again a little closer. . . .

touch push pull intertwine be together

Exactly. And for a little while I am able to really let go and forget that I wish it could never end, but then I do start wishing that it could never end, and then it does. I feel a splash of hot sun on my face, no more leaves to block it, and I hear a car going by close, and Hector stops. I open my eyes and there's the other fence in front of us, and then a ditch and then the road. My house is just up that street and around the corner.

Hector looks at me and I look back, and then we both drop our eyes and we drop each other's hands and step a step away from each other, like we're both all of a sudden really embarrassed. But then he looks at me again, and I see all the complicated layers of yes and no in his face, and I feel more solid than I can ever remember feeling, and I say, "If I tell you, you have to promise not to say anything if . . . if you don't believe me or if you think I'm crazy or something."

"I promise."

I take a deep breath and say, "OK. I don't have a brain tumor. The Procedure is not for that." I swallow, but there's no going back now. "No, what it is is, I have this kind of fourth-dimensional alien person stuck inside me. My dad was a scientist, and I was too close when an experiment went wrong, way back when I was three, and this being got stuck inside me, and now in three days they're going to try to get us unstuck. And . . ." I swallow again, because I'm not sure I'm going to be able to say the last bit, but then I do. "And, there's a pretty good chance it won't work."

His look asks the question.

"And if it doesn't work, that will be the end. Nobody knows what will happen to Zyx, but I'll die." Then I stand there shaking, thinking, Wow, I told. I actually told. It feels so incredibly good.

And Hector says, "I believe you."

....

So we start walking home, I mean, to my house. We don't hold hands anymore, just walk side by side. Our steps fall into a rhythm together and stay that way, and we are close to each other but not touching. That's fine with me. I need a little time inside my own skin again, because of the big tangle of feels roiling around inside me as I prepare to see my family again.

There is one more little bit of talk. Before we get to the corner, Hector says, "Zyx."

"Yeah, Zyx. Short for *zyxilef." He gives me a look at the cork-pop sound and I take a breath to start explaining, but then I think how little time is left before home, so instead I say, "I'll tell you about it some other time."

We walk for another ten steps or so and then he says, "So when you called me stupid, you were talking to Zyx?"

"Yeah."

"And when I said, about you having an alien in your head . . . that was actually true."

"Yeah."

We walk in silence for about ten steps more and then he makes a little noise and I realize he's trying not to laugh, and that makes me laugh, and he laughs, and for the first time we're both laughing together, and it just feels so good like that.

A little more quiet walking and then Hector stops and says, "Um . . . Can I, you know . . . Is he listening right now? Can I talk to him?"

No surprise, that rouses Zyx. My whole body spasms. I say, going along with the "he" and "him"—no time to explain the V-words either—"Yeah, he's always here."

Hector does a laugh-face, like, This is so weird, looking at the same person but talking to someone else, and says, "OK, so, um . . . Hi, Zyx. How's it going?"

This time I practically convulse, and I feel Zyx working in my mouth and throat. I've never felt ven try harder to use my body to speak *not speak sad want answer*

Yeah, you wanted to talk to him. I get that. But all I could do was flail.

Hector steps back a step, but his face stays calm. As soon as I can I say, "He can only talk by typing on a keyboard, but obviously he wants to say hi back." And Hector says, "Cool."

We walk on and somehow we're holding hands again, and sooner than I am ready we turn the corner onto my block, and then we come to my house, and right away—they must have been watching for me—there's Mom on the front porch with Grandy and Bea behind. Mom's hair is flying all over and her fingers are knotted in front of her, and even from the sidewalk I can see that she has been crying, and the coil roil spikes and I almost sit down right there in the street. But nobody does or says anything right away, because Hector is there.

I turn to him and there's a look on his face that for a moment

I think means I've hurt his feelings somehow, but then I realize he's feeling for me. I'm too mixed-up to say or do anything, but he suddenly steps close and kisses me on the cheek—right in the triangle, he kisses me—and then he whispers, "Good luck, Felix . . . Message me after, OK? And, bye Zyx." Then he gives my family a quick look and turns and walks away. He doesn't look back.

So then there's nothing left to do but to walk up the sidewalk and up the steps, and seeing the tears on Mom's face makes my eyes sting too, and then there's a bunch of crying and holding and, you know, the order of who hugged whom and for how long is not important. One thing, though—at some point I realize that nobody's mad at me, and then I realize that the whole time since I left I've had this clenched thing inside of me, this bracing for the impact of everyone being mad at me for running away. But no one is mad, so the clenched thing begins to unclench, and then they ask where I went and I tell them.

Next there's an awkward little stretch—how do you get from everyone on the porch having a big scene to just another Sunday at home with the Yz family? But somehow with little jokes and laughing through hiccups and so on we manage to get inside. The offer of lunch helps, because I'm starving. Also,

Mom thinks of the perfect subject-changing question to ask as we're going in. "That was Hector Dandicat you were with, wasn't it?" I glance at her face and she's still not mad or suspicious or anything, just trying really hard to be casual.

My face goes hot, but Bea saves me the trouble of answering. "Yeah, that was Hector," she says, giving me an X-ray vision look, because of the kiss no doubt.

Mom's brow gets ridges in it. "Was he with you . . ." she says, and waves a hand toward where Portland would be if she was facing the right direction.

"No. He met me at the bus."

"Oh."

I am expecting more questions, but she seems ready to let it go, and then I think I know why, because Ursula is in the kitchen. As soon as I see her, Mom gets all flustery, and I don't know Ursula well enough yet to be sure, but it looks to me like she might be embarrassed, what with how she can't seem to figure out where to point her eyes. She fumbles a coffee cup down onto the counter and says, "Perhaps I should go."

Mom goes to her and lays a hand on her arm for a second and says, "That's probably a good idea—for now. But thank you for stopping by." So then Ursula is making her way out. She still looks embarrassed, but there is the moment when she pauses for a second, going by me, and says, "Felix, if you like, after the Procedure, I will teach you to play chess," and then she's gone.

That takes me a couple of seconds to compute—it's a little involved—and then it's a good thing I take another second to think it all the way through, because my first impulse is to say, "You TOLD?" I mean, I don't actually care that she did, but it has just been so tiresome with Mom constantly harping on the Powers That Be and "Don't tell, don't tell!" Also, she's giving me this look like, Please don't be mad, which I am not, so what I end up saying is, "Not to worry. I told Hector too." And then we all burst out laughing.

The next part is not so fun. Mom does the parenting thing she does and tells me I need to hear how what I did affected the people around me, and then she says they were all really scared for me, especially because they were afraid that if they told anyone I had run away, the Powers would mobilize the National Guard or whatever to look for me, so they couldn't even call the police. All they could do was sit at home and worry and hope I'd come back. So then I feel really bad because of how much I scared my family.

Then we have to talk about how tomorrow it's going to be time to go to the Facility, and the weight of everything falls down on me again like an enormous boulder, and the conversation gets bumpy. It seems so close all of a sudden—not close even, already here—and I don't feel ready, so I get tense. "Can't we have just one more day of regular life?" I say. Mom gets tense too, and Bea goes and starts playing the piano. Only Grandy stays calm, in that irritating way of veirs. But it's not too bad, really. The feels of the porch are still there, so somehow we get through it.

And, here's Mom, standing in the door of my room again. I should say, I came up here with orders to pack, but I've been writing this instead.

Me: "I'm typing what we're saying again."

Her: "OK."

Me: long silence, like, What?

"Felix, I just spoke with Dr. Yoon on the phone, and she says that, if we want, we can take one more day at home before we go in. It's not ideal, but it's doable. So I thought, let's get out of our house and our lives, off this track we're on, for just a day, and go do something fun. Together. All of us."

I flop my mouth at her for a second and then say, "OK. Sure."

She smiles. "Good." She twiddles her hair for a second. "It's too bad we didn't think of this sooner—we could have made more elaborate plans. As it is, we're limited to where we can get to and back from in a day, and of course the Powers have to sign off on your choice, but Dr. Yoon says she can arrange that within reason. So, what do you want to do, sweetheart? Where do you want to go?"

The answer is right there. "I want to go somewhere where I can hear some jazz," I say.

She blinks. "Jazz?" she says. Then she waggles her head and says, "Well, all right. That sounds like fun. I'm not sure . . . I'll have to do some research. But let's see what we can find."

I nod, and she comes into the room and puts her hand on my shoulder and kisses my forehead, and coils and roils and all that, I put my head down, but it's fine.

So how about that? Jazz. Maybe she'll find Steven's band. Wouldn't that be great? I could say "Hey," and he would say "Hey," and then everyone would wonder how I knew him.

jazz pretty

Yeah, jazz pretty. Those records—it was like what you showed me, sorta. Getting lost in the patterns, with time always going underneath, making it all run.

yes

OK, so maybe in three days I'll be dead, but I'm going on a field trip tomorrow. Another one, I mean, here in three dimensions. So, my life isn't over quite yet.

2 Days to Go

For once, typing that doesn't fill me all the way up with dread. Mostly, but not fully. Because, we're on the train to Boston to hear some jazz. Field trip! And, btw, it's a lot nicer to be inside the train than sitting out in the wind.

We got a set of four seats facing each other in pairs. I've got the window facing forward, and it's so cool watching the scenery go by, all those backyards and bus parking lots and loading docks. I have the laptop on my lap. Bea is next to me, and Mom and Grandy (in skirt and panty hose, it being Monday) are across from us. OK, no particular reason why, but I'm going to type whatever anybody says, just to capture a little bit of real life. [Note added right after: The talk happened too fast to catch it all, so I filled in the rest after with Zyx helping, and added these bracket notes too.]

Bea: You know what would be cool, in a sick sort of way? If you saw a murder happening in a backyard as you went by. Good setup for a detective novel.

Grandy: I feel certain that it has been used, though I cannot immediately cite a reference.

Bea: Like, just as the train goes by, you see one person pointing a gun, and then the flash of the gun going off, and the other person starts to crumple to the ground, and then, zoop!, you're past it.

Me: And you're the only one who saw it—

Bea: Yeah, and maybe the person with the gun was disguised somehow . . . something odd—

Mom: A mask, perhaps—

Me: Yeah, a clown mask!

Grandy: Overused, I fear.

Me: OK, how about a full-head monster mask? Something green and yellow with lots of bumps and teeth on it?

Grandy: Less used.

Bea: And then you search online and you can't find any mention of it anywhere, but you become obsessed and start investigating yourself. You figure out which two stations you were between and you start snooping around—

Me: And . . . hey, are there cookies in there? [Grandy has pulled out the tote bag of snacks vo has brought.]

Grandy: Indeed there are. [hands me a couple of ginger snaps]

Mom: And what's in that thermos? [top sticking out of bag] Coffee?

Grandy: No, dearheart, it's tea.

Mom: Really?

Grandy: Anagram of "tock."

Bea: Say again?

Grandy: Anagram of "tock." [Grandy has this thing about making up word puzzles. We're all used to it, so we all know that that's what this is, and all three of us start thinking aloud—This one's hard, I don't get it, stuff like that.]

Bea: I give up.

Grandy: [handing the filled cup lid to Mom] Tea. See? OK?

[all three of us groaning and complaining, Grandy smiling that cat-smile of veirs]

Me: Oh, sorry, crumbs on the keyboard.

Mom: Well, honey, just blow them off gently.

Bea: Hey, do you remember? Cone full of jimmies? [Nelson, this is taking a lot of explaining. She's talking about something that happened a couple of summers ago at the lake. She asked for a cone completely full of jimmies, and the ice cream person gave it to her.]

Bea: [laughing, talking to me] I kept throwing them at you, but only one at a time, and they were so small you couldn't feel them, and pretty soon your hair was full of candy sprinkles.

Mom: [in her dry Mom voice] Which melted when we tried to wash them out. Should have used cold water.

Grandy: Should have just jumped in the lake.

Bea: The cone got gross by the second day, though. I put it in the freezer, and the jimmies all kinda stuck together in a mass. It was like a psychedelic baby hedgehog died in there.

Grandy: Psychedelic baby hedgehog. Excellent.

Me: I like jimmies.

Mom: They are very colorful, aren't they? And very nibblable.

Grandy: [bouncing a little and grinning, which vo does when vo has thought of something vo's really pleased with] Inimitably nibblable!

All right, I guess that's enough. That's what it's like all the time at our house. Zyx, I'm surprised that you can understand anything at all.

understand love

Oh gack. You didn't.

is true

Yeah, OK, whatever.

Still 2 Days to Go

Now it is late night again, and we're home, and I'm just typing a little about how the rest of the day went before I go to sleep.

All that there really is to say is that we had fun. All of us together. We walked through the Common and it was really warm and some of the trees were starting to leaf out. Then we had dinner in a fancy restaurant with a candle on the table and I had this amazing dessert, a piece of chocolate cake, which compared to chocolate cake I have had before was like a real volcano next to a science-fair volcano. It had this huge orange flower on it—Mom said it was a daylily—and they had dusted confectioners' sugar over it, so when you picked the flower up, its shadow was left behind. The flower, the shadow of the flower, and the sugar between—threes everywhere! And the person who waited on us said I could eat the flower, so I did, and it tasted like pepper.

Then we went to this club that Mom had found on the 'net, and there was a hassle at the door because the guy said that Bea and I were too young to get in, but Grandy did this thing like out of a movie where vo took the guy over to the side and whispered to him and actually handed him a bill, and the guy came back and let us in and when I passed him he gave me a look and a nod, so I knew Grandy must have told him the Story. Which bugged me for a second, but then I thought, Hey, for why we're here, it's true.

We sat at a little table with another candle on it, and Mom and Grandy had drinks and Bea and I had soft drinks, and then the band came out. There were four of them: piano, bass, drums, and sax. They sat down and shuffled around and the sax player tooted and bleeped a little and fiddled with her mouthpiece, and then they looked at each other and did a big nod all together and started to play.

And now I have sat here for five minutes without being able to say anything about the music. Actually, what I've been doing is, and I wish there was a way to type this, I've been singing saxophone, and Zyx has been playing drums with my hands. Which I guess makes us a duo. Cool.

jazz pretty

Yep, maybe that's all there is to say. Except it's so much more than that. It was like, there were all these different colors in the air. And the four musicians, they were talking to each other through the music, and sometimes they were all serious, but other times they were actually telling jokes. I've never laughed at music before. I mean, laughed because it was funny. But it was funny.

You know, the black and red, they're still down in here somewhere. But now it's like there's also a separate inner me, standing on an empty plain under a dark sky in the middle of my soul, but not minding, because I'm playing a sax solo, and I'm grooving on it, and it just feels so sweet to be down inside the music like that.

OK, I almost erased that last sentence, thinking, *eye-roll*, but no. I wrote it, and there it is, and there it is going to stay.

Oh, and speaking of writing, I forgot to mention, Mom's phone rang while we were walking across the Common, and it was Ms. C calling to say that my threeness essay won first prize in the essay contest. I made a really loud whoop! noise and did a victory dance, which my family joined me in, so we were all hopping around under the trees.

The awards ceremony is in two weeks. Even with the black and red constantly lurking around, that makes me laugh.

And one other thing. I checked Novaglyph just now, and I can't tell for sure, but I think maybe Ash put me in the comic. Just a figure in the background, walking, but it looks like me— all hunched over, and the hair and clothes are right. And I'm pretty sure her turnaround is only about a week, so it has been long enough. If she did, Nelson, how cool is that? But also, people could still be looking at the picture when . . . when . . . no. Not going there. Not. Going. There.

Not.

It's really really late. I have to sleep now. How can I? But, yeah, I'm tired. Sleep.

1 Day to Go

Tomorrow is ZeroDay.

So what I'm doing now is, I'm typing because it's something different to do besides freak and bolt.

I am all by myself in a hospital room, dressed in one of those closes-in-the-back robes, and I'm hungry and thirsty because I haven't had anything to eat or drink except little measured-out amounts of water since this morning, and I'm lonely. Lonely. How can such strong feels fit inside one word? I'm lonely because I had to say good-bye to Grandy and Bea and Mom. I'm not going to see them again until after . . . if . . .

And, I'm back. What's the use of crying? This is going to happen. There's no stopping it now. Keep calm, Felix. Write.

Yes, I am lonely. I am also completely hairless. Zoe, this really nice nurse, put an extra sheet on my bed, which is one of those fancy hospital beds that they've scrunched up so it's like being in my chair, and then she had me take off all my clothes and lie down, and she put another sheet over me. Then she uncovered different parts of me again and calmly shaved off every hair on my entire body. She saved the parts parts for last and I thought I would be horribly embarrassed, but she was so business-as-usual about it, it wasn't so bad. I looked in the mirror after, and I look like a nine-year-old war orphan or something, all smooth and pale. And my face without eyebrows looks like someone else's face, and now the sheets feel slippery. It's strange.

Anyway.

So we had to get up super early again because of taking the extra day for the field trip. I felt like I had only just gotten to sleep when Mom shook my shoulder, but I cracked through the pain of the Pose—no lockup for several days now, although this morning was close—and pulled on some clothes and zombie-shuffled out to the car. It was still completely dark. I buckled myself in and fell back asleep and didn't wake up until we stopped for gas, by which point the sun was well up. The sky was hazy white and the sun was like the pimple of greatest glare in a giant ocean of glare, and, Mother Hubbard, my brain is tired. We got to the Facility right on time. Gate up, drive in, park, and then they took us to the apartment where Mom and Grandy and Bea are staying while this happens, and me too when it is over.

Yeah, when. No "if" this time. What's the point? We all know it's there, so why keep saying it? That "if" up there near the start of this entry, that's the last one.

So then we just had to hang out for a while. Everyone was hungry, but they were waiting until Dr. Yoon came to take me away for tests so that I wouldn't have to sit there watching them eat. I wasn't allowed to eat anything myself, so that was nice of them. There were a few games and such, including a jigsaw puzzle, brand-new, shrink-wrap still on the box. It was a picture of a house in the Netherlands with a boat and a windmill. Bea and I broke it open and started sorting out the straight edges, arguing about who was going to get to do the vanes of the windmill. Grandy sat and read, and Mom unpacked and fussed around, sitting down and then getting up and sitting down again somewhere else, all the time tying her fingers into knots. Finally she came over and helped sort pieces. Then Dr. Yoon was there and I had to go.

This was just a checkup, not the having-to-say-good-bye part yet, so I went with her and got poked and probed and sampled. It was on the no-fun side of boring, except everyone was really kind, especially Dr. Yoon.

So, tests done, I get back to the apartment, and they've had lunch and cleaned up everything after, except someone forgot a carton of orange juice on the counter and when I see it my mouth goes Sproing! and Bea whisks it into the fridge with a "sorry" look. I give her back an "it's OK" nod. We all know this is how it has to be.

Then, more hanging out, waiting. We get the straight edges done except for one we missed, over in the trees on the right side. It bugs me, but I don't want to go back through all thousand pieces again looking for it, or whatever's left of the thousand, anyway, after all but one of the straight edges are taken out. And then Dr. Yoon is there again and says gently, "Felix, it's almost time. I'll be back in about five minutes, and then we have to go," and she steps out again.

So I stand up from the puzzle table, and everyone else stands up too, and there's this awkward moment while we all stand there looking at each other, and then Grandy comes over without saying anything and wraps veir arms around me and holds me tight. Vo's in Vera mode, it being Tuesday, and the ruffles on veir blouse tickle the side of my face. I can feel from veir body that vo is crying . . . I am crying . . . just assume there's lots of crying, OK? After a bit vo holds me apart again a little, veir hands on my shoulders, and says, "Vercingetorix."

"What?"

"Vercingetorix. That's what my parents named me."

I have no idea how to put all the feels I am feeling into words, so what I say is, "What kind of name is that?" Not mean—just asking.

"It's the name of a famous Gaulish chieftain who threw down his arms at Julius Caesar's feet after he was defeated by the power and glory that was Rome."

"So . . . so you're an Yz by birth."

"Yes."

"And you were born a boy."

"I was born with a male body, yes."

"You're my father's father."

"Biologically speaking, yes."

We look at each other, and then I drop my eyes because I suddenly feel, I don't know, embarrassed? Bashful? It's weird.

Vo says softly, "Father, mother, parent. Does it really matter?"

I look back up. "No. Not really." Vo takes me in veir arms again and we hold each other another little time, and then I think of something and say, "Um, tomorrow is Wednesday, right?"

"Yes."

"Your day . . . What about your day? Will you . . . ?"

"Don't worry, I'll be there."

Not that it matters—really, it doesn't—but I still can't help the questioning look.

Grandy smiles sadly and says, "Vera. In the end, if I had to choose for good and all, I think it would be Vera. But luckily I don't have to choose." Then, "I love you, Felix. Good luck."

I've always had a hard time actually saying those words, but this time it's easy. "I love you too."

Vo nods, then tips veir head a little to one side and says, "Good-bye, *zyxilef. We'll miss you." And Zyx makes me twitch, just once.

You wanted to say good-bye.

yes

Or you did say good-bye. That was your way of saying it.

yes

Yes. So then Grandy steps away, and it's Bea's turn.

This is getting harder and harder to write about.

OK, so mostly just hugs and wet cheeks, not much talking. The last thing she says is: "You better not die in that machine, little brother. If you die, I'm going to kill you."

And then Mom . . . and you know what, never mind writing about that. And then Dr. Yoon comes in again with Zoe and a wheelchair, and they tell me to sit down and then they wheel me away.

So then the full-body shave I already described, and this other business to clear out my insides, which was gross and painful and which I really don't need to go into detail about. Then Zoe comes in with a pill and says I have to take it to help me sleep, and I say, Wait a minute, I have to do my writing, and she says OK, but it has to be soon, so I have been typing this as fast as I can.

The only other thing is Hector. I want so bad to open a window and see if he's there, but I can't quite make myself do it. I keep hovering the cursor, but he said, "Message me after," so it feels awkward. And anyway, I feel like I'm not in that world anymore. I feel like if I reconnect, I might completely fall apart. So, better not.

I asked them to wake me up early enough so I can type one more time before the Procedure, so, one more entry after this. And I asked Bea to record what actually happens—she has a little handheld recorder she uses when she practices. So after, depending . . . well, either I'll type it out, or someone else might. So, that will be here.

Zyx, how are you doing?

question mark

How do you feel?

feel here now always

Doesn't anything get you down, ever?

not understand

Never mind. Are you ready?

yes

I guess I am too. Ready as I'll ever be. OK, Zoe is back. Time to take this pill. Good night.

ZeroDay

Up until now I haven't really been too worried about how much it has been starting to hurt in the morning. There was that one lockup I couldn't get out of by myself, but then it seemed to get better again.

Just now was different. I woke up because Dr. Yoon was shaking my shoulder and calling my name. I made a noise and I felt her hand go away again, leaving me lying there, trying to get my brain to work. It was like no time had passed since I'd closed my eyes. I felt stupid and heavy. The pill, I guess. Head full of cotton balls.

After a minute I went to push aside the covers, and I realized I couldn't move. At all. My whole body felt jammed, and then it started to hurt, more and more, quickly. It felt like a giant steel spring winding tighter and tighter, knotting all my muscles up, and pretty soon I was going to shatter into thousands of bloody shards. I tried to call for help, but my throat was locked, and all of a sudden even breathing felt like lifting the back end of a car.

Then a moment came when I couldn't breathe at all, and I felt my heart lurch in my chest, like the next time it wasn't going to be able to beat. And then . . . well, then it got a little better again. I don't know why. I scraped in a breath, and another, and my muscles unwound enough that I was able to move. And my heart kept beating, obviously, but each beat felt like someone hitting me on the sternum with a hammer—still does—and I was shaking and covered with sweat and everything hurt. Zyx, you must have felt that, right?

yes

Do you know what it was?

not know how say

But you know.

. . .

Gah, sometimes I wish you were better at words. Are you OK?
Did it hurt you too?

no yes

You mean no, you're not OK, and yes, it hurt?

yes

You've never said that before. Never said anything about pain
or hurt.

stuck not dance

I don't know what you mean.

stuck not dance no joy zyx hold now procedure now

Um, do I understand you right? You're doing something to
keep me alive?

yes

And it hurts?

not dance

And you need the Procedure to happen as soon as possible.

yes

Um, OK. Hang on.

. . .

We can't rush it, but we're almost there.

. . .

Um, yeah. Fast as we can.

And, there's not much left to tell. Dr. Yoon didn't come back, but the nurse did. It's not Zoe, it's the nurse from the final fitting. Nidal. He's nice, but I wish Zoe were here. He just made me go to the bathroom one last time, even though I had almost nothing to go, and then he said he's coming back in a minute to give me a shot that will make me start to go to sleep, and then they will wheel me out and put me in the Apparatus and give me another shot to knock me out, and then I will either wake up again or I won't.

How can words possibly . . .

Simple. Just say.

I'm scared of dying.

And I'm scared of not dying. I'm scared of waking up and Zyx being gone. I don't know if I can do it. I don't know if I can live without ven. Just live like any other kid. Zyx, what am I going to do without you?

live dance do be joy

Yes. That's right. I want to try. I want to live. I want so badly to live. I want to take saxophone lessons. I want to learn to play chess, for real this time. I want to throw a straw at Bea the next time she needs it—she always has for me. I want to take Hector on a trust walk. I want to finish Jarq. I want to live.

So. Zyx. I guess this is good-bye.

yes

And, um . . . I don't think I've ever said this before. Sorry. Zyx, I'm sorry.

question mark

I'm so sorry. Not just for your pain now. For everything. For my dad doing what he did. Getting us stuck. I can't imagine what it's been like for you. And, gah, I can't see to type, and there's no time to go into the bathroom.

no worries

No fair, stop making me laugh!

question mark

Nelson. Mother Hubbard. Zyx. I'm going to miss you so much.

here now all one all times

Yeah, I know, we're all interconnected in the infinite afterglow tracery web of the hurtling Is particle.

yes

And that was your last chance to understand sarcasm. Hopeless.

. . .

Or maybe it's not sarcasm. Because, I do feel that in some way you'll always be with me.

yes

Yes. OK. Good-bye.

. . .

Thank you.

. . .

Zyx, I love you.

zyx love felix

Yes.

OK.

Bye.

I want my mom. And I want my dad. I wish so bad he was still alive. And you know what? When Hector kissed me, I should have kissed him back. I should have told him that I love him, too, right there in front of the house.

Well, I'll just have to tell him after. Here's Nidal.

ZeroMoment

Hi, this is Beatrix Yz, reporting for Felix about the Procedure that is about to happen, and we are in a little room high up in the wall of the big square chamber where the Apparatus is, and in a minute they're going to bring Felix out and put him in it. Oh, you better come out of this all right, little brother.

Now a technician person is here and . . . hold on, I'll be right back.

OK, I'm back. The technician person was just explaining that we need to wear these big headphones, but not so we can hear. It's to protect our hearing, because the amount of electricity that is going to go through the Apparatus at the ZeroMoment is like a hundred bolts of lightning and there is going to be the thunder of a hundred bolts of lightning. Also, when the

ZeroMoment happens, we're supposed to crouch down behind these metal shields on the other side of the room from the window in case it breaks. The window is a foot thick, and it's weird to look through because even though it's clear, it has this subtle green-blue color, so everything on the other side looks like it's underwater.

Oh, I'm scared, but I have to keep recording because I promised Felix I would. And now what? Grandy is singing?

> Feels
> Feels with wheels

Mom's got the middle part. That leaves the high line for me.

> Over you it steals
> This feeling of feels
> Oh, those feels
> Sneak into your heart
> Tear it all apart
> Leave you gasping and sore
> But wanting more
> More feels
> Feels . . . with . . . wheels

There you go, Felix. A final threeness for luck.

And, here he is. The door is opening, and here comes a little group. Dr. Yoon is there, and Dr. Gordon, and two other people, nurses, I guess, or technicians, and Felix in a wheelchair, wearing a hospital robe. Now he's getting up, and he looks like he must be drugged, because he almost fell down, and they're holding him up.

Now they're taking the robe off him, and oh, he looks like a pathetic little vulnerable Gumby thing, no hair, not even eyebrows . . . Little brother, don't die . . . OK, I have to stay strong and keep talking . . .

So now he's sort of trying to help, but mostly they're doing it, they're slathering the goo all over him, and now he's all shiny and slippery-looking, and they're helping him up the steps. He's going really slowly. . . . Oh, I have to turn off the recorder again.

OK, that took about ten minutes, but they finally got him all down inside, just his face still peeking out, like a baby bird inside an egg, and now they've closed the egg again. There's a hatch that closes and latches, and he's all down inside there now, breathing through a tube.

Just before they closed the hatch, they reached in and gave him another shot, so he's asleep now, and in the next minute or two the machine is going to rev up. . . . Actually, we can already hear the hum of it getting louder. . . . I guess it has to build up for a long time for the big zap. And now they're going to stop his heart and . . . and . . . oh, this is terrible . . . they're going to stop his heart, and then the zap will happen, and then the machine will start his heart again, and then they'll run in in case it doesn't, and then . . . then it will be done. One way or another, it will be done.

OK, it's time. Here we go. The humming is getting louder now, it's building up, the electricity is building up, and there's kind of a glowy haze around the Apparatus, and it's getting brighter and it's getting louder in here. . . . I have to put my headphones on now, and we're getting down behind the metal barrier. I can't see the Apparatus anymore, but the hum is getting louder. . . . It's getting really loud in here and really bright. . . . [twenty seconds of static, sound of explosion]

OK, I guess it's done. There was a huge flash and a clap of thunder that hurt my ears even with the headphones on, and the whole room shook. The hum is getting quieter again, and we're up and looking through the window and the people are running in, they're running up the stairs, they're opening . . . I saw Felix's face for just a second, it looked all white and still . . . oh, and, um, they're pulling him out, they're checking . . . and thumbs up, thumbs up! He's alive, he's alive! I gotta go.

Zyx?

Zyx? Are you there?

Mother Hubbard, I thought I would be done crying. I guess not. Excuse me, I'll be back in a minute.

And, I'm back. And, it worked, obviously. I woke up about an hour ago, but this is the first chance I've had to write, what with feels and tests and washing the goop off.

Before I tell about waking up, there's something else I want to capture right away, because I can feel it already fading, the way dreams fade. It wasn't a dream, though, at least not like any dream I've had before. More like the field trip to the fourth dimension that Zyx gave me, but not quite like that, either. Halfway in between, I guess. And it's strange that it happened, because I was drugged and then dead and then still drugged, but it did.

What happened was, I found myself floating in a golden place, and I felt no fear, only warmth and peace. It didn't occur to me to try to figure out if I had a body or not. There was a kind of feeling of music that was actually a color that tasted the way lavender smells, and that makes no sense, but that's what it was like.

Zyx was there. I could feel ven stronger and more clearly than ever before, except I was the one inside and vo was the one who was all around. Then the gold began to swirl, and I began to see faces around me, then bodies. They stood or floated a little way away, looking at me with calm eyes. The one in front was a tall skinny boy with dark hair who I knew as soon as I saw him must be my brother, Ben, and behind him was my dad, looking older than the pictures I've seen, and then, spreading out behind them, more faces and bodies going back into the hazy distance. They did not smile. They looked at me as though through glass. It felt sad, but sweet too.

Then the swirling picked up speed and black started to mix in with the gold. The faces and bodies went away, not snuffed out or anything scary like that, just swept away in the swirling. And the black, it wasn't scary either. It was a soft silk black that in a weird way felt as comforting as the gold, like the necessary other half of it. The swirling got faster and faster and the gold spun down to a thread, an endless golden thread that twisted around itself, spirals within spirals within spirals, and even though the thread had no thickness, there was so much of it twisted and swirled every which way that it still filled all the space I was in. And I felt that one part of the thread was twisted around in the shape of me, and that another part off in the dark somewhere, an infinity of nested spirals away, but still connected, was twisted around in the shape of Zyx.

Then I did feel like I had a body, including closed eyes I could open, so I opened them.

Everyone was there, Mom and Bea and Grandy and Dr. Yoon and Dr. Gordon. Mom squeezed me so tight I could hardly breathe, and Grandy said a thing about the phoelix rising from the ashes (vo specifically mentioned to spell it that way . . . I roll my eyes), and Bea actually gave me a kiss. I don't know if she's ever done that before, since I was a baby, at least, but it was nice.

And I keep stretching, because I finally can. I can stretch my arms over my head all the way from the big shoulder joints to the fingertips at the same time that I stretch my legs all the way down to my toes, and it crackles all down my spine and it feels totally amazing. Wait a second, I'm going to do it again.

Oh, Nelson, that feels so GOOD. I didn't know how hard it

was to move, before. And look, my hands aren't jerking at all. And when I talk, the words come flowing out as fast as I think them. I can talk. I can move. I'm free.

Zyx, I hope you're all right, back there in your fourth dimension. I hope you're dancing free. I'm going to miss you. And thanks, again. Thanks for holding me together in the last little bit, and for everything else. Thanks, and sorry, and bye.

So now what?

Um, well, now I can go get my award for the writing contest. Two hundred dollars, not bad. And when I read part of my essay aloud at the ceremony like Ms. C said, I'll actually be able to read it. And maybe I can use the prize money to buy a used saxophone. And now I can really get to work on drawing Jarq, and writing it too. And . . . wait, hold on. Chat window. It's Hector. Hey, he didn't wait, he messaged first. Cool. I'll be right back.

29 Days Ago

How can a month have gone by already?

I had an idea that I might keep writing entries here, because even in the middle of all the feels and drama and stuff, I was having more and more fun putting what was happening into words, but I've just been so busy.

Yeah, a LOT has been going on. Where to even start? Well, Hector and I are making a comic together now. Turns out he draws way better than I do, so I'm doing the story and he's doing the art. So far our comic is called Squodylax, which is this weird random word Hector came up with, and honestly I don't like it but I haven't figured out yet how to say that. Even with the not-so-good name, though, it is wicked fun working with him. We pass rough draft pages back and forth between classes. Like, I do an outline-y thing in first period and hand it to him at the corner by the door to the cafeteria where we always pass, and by third period he's got a pencil sketch that he's waiting at the same corner to hand back to me, with voice balloons ready to be filled in, and then, well, I won't go into all the details, but it's cool. And I'm actually glad to give Jarq a rest. Not done with it, just letting it sit for a bit.

Other than the comic, I'm not sure exactly what's going on with Hector. The first week or two after I got back to school, until last week actually, there was so much fuss about me seeming so different to everyone and still having no eyebrows and stuff that I didn't get to talk to him hardly at all, and now if I try to talk to him about anything but Squodylax it gets awkward, because without the extra push of maybe being about to die it feels complicated. To tell the truth, I have no idea what I'm doing. So, we talk about Squodylax a lot.

Maybe we're just comic-drawing friends now?

Maybe. But then there's also the part where the other day Mom suggested that when we go to the lake this summer we could ask Hector if he wants to come with us, and my brain just kind of froze up, because, Hector at the lake. Gooooonnnnnnggggg! Hector at the lake. I haven't asked him. I got close once, but at the last second my tongue got gluey. I still have a few weeks before summer. I wonder if I will. I really don't know if I'm going to be able to make myself do it. Gooooonnnnnggggg!

Oh, and the other thing at school that's truly freaky, aside from the general freakiness of everyone wanting to gush at me all the time, is Tim. He keeps talking to me, and I think maybe, I mean, I can't believe it, but I think he's trying to make friends? Which means I'm having to work just as hard as I was before to avoid him. Gah.

What else, since I seem to be summing up? Well, turns out Mom and Ursula in the sunroom after dinner is just as squirmworthy as Mom and Rick was—exactly the same—so nothing has changed there. And Grandy's the same as ever, still smiling that cat smile of veirs, and Ursula tried to teach me chess, but I decided without Zyx it was too hard, and sax is hard too, but I can't seem to stop trying again, and, um, let's see. . . . the awards ceremony went fine . . . and Bea had her big spring recital and even without Zyx I felt the music move me. It was really different hearing her play the big black piano up on the stage, even though I've been listening to her practice all the pieces for months. Including the sinfonias. Three of them, actually. How about that? A threeness of threenesses. The nineness of things! Or not. There's no end in that direction. Probably best to leave that alone.

And then, no more Zyx. I still get sad about that, but then the golden thread vision-dream comes back into my mind and I feel a little better, because I can sense vo and I are still connected. No way to say hey, but still connected.

So, as I was saying, I thought I'd keep writing here, but I'm not sure I will after all. Maybe I'm too busy living to write about living. Every day, I mean, here in this journal. I'm writing Squodylax, and I'll get back to writing Jarq, and beyond that I feel like I could choose any little section of that infinite golden spiral to focus in on and it would turn out to be another story that wants to be told. There's no end of writing to be done. Maybe just not this one particular way anymore.

Zyx, whadayathink? Any reason I shouldn't just live as hard as I can, every second, and not worry about catching it all? Because who needs to catch it when you're right there in the middle of it, doing it, being it, living it? Any reason at all?

Yep, I agree. That's what I think too. Let's go.